ERNEST HEMINGWAY

THE LIFE AND THE LEGEND

Frontis: Ernest selected an informal photo for his publicity picture in the 1920s. (Charles Scribner's Sons)

ERNEST HEMINGWAY

THE LIFE AND THE LEGEND

Richard B. Lyttle

Illustrated with photographs

ATHENEUM · 1992 · NEW YORK

Maxwell Macmillan Canada
TORONTO

Maxwell Macmillan International
NEW YORK   OXFORD   SINGAPORE   SYDNEY

Atheneum
Macmillan Publishing Company
866 Third Avenue
New York, NY 10022

Maxwell Macmillan Canada, Inc.
1200 Eglinton Avenue East
Suite 200
Don Mills, Ontario M3C 3N1

Macmillan Publishing Company is part of
the Maxwell Communication Group of
Companies.

First Edition

Printed in the United States of America

1 2 3 4 5 6 7 8 9 10

Book design by Patrice Fodero

Maps by Richard B. Lyttle

Library of Congress Cataloging-in-Publication Data
Lyttle, Richard B.
     Ernest Hemingway: the life and the legend/by Rich-
ard B. Lyttle; illustrated with photographs and with maps
by the author.—1st ed.
          p.   cm.
     Includes bibliographical references and index.
     Summary: Studies the life and works of the twen-
tieth-century American author, describing the childhood and adult experiences that became common
themes in many of his stories and novels.
     ISBN 0–689–31670–4
     1. Hemingway, Ernest, 1899–1961—Biography—
Juvenile literature. 2. Authors, American—20th century—Biography—Juvenile literature. [1. Hemingway, Ernest, 1899–1961. 2. Authors, American.]
I. Title.
PS3515.E37Z697   1992
813′.52—dc20
     [B]   91–11218

This book is for

Logan Franklin

Contents

PROLOGUE: THE LIFE AND THE LEGEND   xi

1. EARLY YEARS   3

2. THE TEENAGER   11

3. THE GREAT ADVENTURE   19

4. THE HERO'S RETURN   33

5. HADLEY   39

6. CHANGING FORTUNES   46

7. IN OUR TIME   53

8. THE NOVELIST   60

9. PAULINE   68

10. KEY WEST   75

11. THE BROKEN ARM   83

12. CUBA   91

CONTENTS

13. AFRICA   98

14. BIMINI   105

15. OFF TO WAR   111

16. DATELINE MADRID   119

17. MARTY   126

18. FOR WHOM THE BELL TOLLS   133

19. WAR AGAIN   141

20. WITH THE INFANTRY   148

21. MARY   155

22. ITALY REVISITED   163

23. THE OLD MAN AND THE SEA   171

24. REPORTED DEAD   178

25. PARIS MEMOIRS   188

26. FINAL DAYS   195

    EPILOGUE   204

    SELECT BIBLIOGRAPHY   205

    INDEX   207

The Life and the Legend

EVERYTHING HE WROTE, ERNEST HEMINGWAY ONCE said, was based on experience; and few men have experienced so much. He was a cub reporter in Kansas City, an ambulance driver in Italy in World War I, and an expatriate in Paris after the war. He was a hunter, a deep-sea fisherman, and an amateur boxer. As a war correspondent, he covered the Spanish civil war and the fighting in China and Europe in World War II. He was decorated for heroism by three governments.

He could speak several languages. His friends included bullfighters, sports heroes, soldiers, ranch hands, artists, and movie idols.

Hemingway's novels and short stories won him global fame largely because they were based on his own adventurous life. Few authors before or since have received as much public attention. He became a legend. His name still stands for strength, tough manhood, and cool courage under stress. His forceful, terse style, unique at the time and very much a part of the "tough guy" legend, still influences writers everywhere.

Behind the legend, however, was a complex man. As a friend, he could be unpredictable and difficult. Although physically active, he was almost pathetically clumsy. He suffered dark, self-destructive moods. His relations with women were stormy. When he was writing, the words sometimes flowed, but more often he agonized over his work.

Quite clearly, Hemingway the legend and Hemingway the man are two very different personalities. By following Hemingway through his many adventures, we see that the contrast between the legend and the man is perhaps the most fascinating part of his story.

ERNEST HEMINGWAY

THE LIFE AND THE LEGEND

A family portrait taken in 1903 shows Dr. and Mrs. Hemingway with Ernest sitting between two sisters, Ursula on the left and Marcelline on the right. (Hemingway Society)

Chapter 1

Early Years

THE BABY WEIGHED NINE AND A HALF POUNDS AND
was just an inch short of two feet. He had a strong cry which
his parents agreed was definitely a boy's cry. The Hemingways
had wanted a boy.

Ernest Miller Hemingway was born at 8:00 A.M., July 21,
1899, in the front bedroom of grandfather Ernest Hall's house
in Oak Park, Illinois, a wealthy suburb of Chicago. The baby
was Dr. Clarence Edmonds and Grace Hall Hemingway's second child. Their first, Marcelline, had been born eighteen
months earlier.

Dr. Hemingway, known to his friends as Ed, was a sturdy
six-footer with a black beard, a sharp Roman nose, and brown
eyes. He had earned his degree at Rush Medical College in
Chicago, toured Europe, and in 1895 returned to Oak Park
to open a general practice. He collected stamps, coins, arrow-
heads, and small birds and animals that he stuffed himself. He
also had preserved a variety of snakes in jars of alcohol. He
loved camping, hunting, and fishing and was eager to introduce
the outdoor world to his son.

Ed Hemingway and Grace Hall met in high school days.

Both were Protestants with small tolerance for other faiths. Grace was a large woman with light brown hair, a creamy complexion, eyes of china blue, and an excellent contralto voice. She had hoped for a career in opera, but in her youth scarlet fever had left her eyes permanently sensitive to strong light. Although she studied at the Art Students League in New York, she gave up hope of a singing career when she discovered that stage lights were too strong for her eyes.

Her plan was to returned to Oak Park, live with her father, Ernest Hall, by then a widower, and teach music; but on October 1, 1896, soon after returning from a tour of Europe, she married young Dr. Hemingway. They began married life in Ernest Hall's large house at 439 North Oak Park Avenue. Dr. Hemingway's parents, Anson and Adelaide Hemingway, lived across the street.

Both of the new baby's grandfathers were veterans of the Civil War, and both had successful businesses in Chicago. Ernest Hall's company made cutlery. Anson Hemingway headed a large real estate firm.

The baby prospered as well. Young Ernest, calm and healthy, had his father's brown eyes and his mother's light brown hair.

The Hemingways spent their summers in a rustic cottage on Walloon Lake , in Charlevoix County, Michigan, not far from the town of Petoskey. They cooked on a wood-burning kitchen stove, got water by working an iron pump handle, and read by the light of oil lamps. Windemere Cottage, as Grace called it, had two small bedrooms, a kitchen, a cramped dining room, and a large front room with a big fireplace flanked by two windows that looked onto the lake.

During his first summer at Windemere in 1900, young Ernest began to walk and talk. He and Marcelline, playing naked in the summer sun, spent hours crawling in and out of the family rowboat that lay beached in the shallow water below the cottage. Ernest did not cry often, but he could roar with rage if Marcelline ever took one of his toys.

He loved words, listened avidly to stories, and cherished picture books that showed animals or birds he could name. Words had magic. When his mother knelt down with him at night beside his bed, Ernest discovered that he could end prayers anytime he wished by shouting "Amen" and jumping under the covers.

His hopes for a baby brother were thwarted when Ursula arrived in April of 1902.

Michigan summers gave Ernest a love for nature. He could name most common flowers, birds, and insects. At age three, when he went on his first fishing trip with his father, he caught the biggest fish.

His friendship with Wesley Dilworth began in the summer of 1903 when Ernest was four. The Dilworths lived in Horton Bay on the shores of Lake Charlevoix, two miles west of Windemere. The father was a blacksmith and the mother ran Pinehurst Cottage, a restaurant with a view of the lake. The friendship with the Dilworths lasted through Ernest's childhood, and the Lake Charlevoix region became as familiar to him as the country around Walloon Lake .

In Oak Park in the fall of 1903, Ernest entered kindergarten and joined a nature club his father had organized. Every Saturday morning, club members hiked the woods to collect nature specimens. After Grandfather Hall gave Ernest a microscope, the boy spent hours with his collections.

On November 28, 1904, another sister, Madelaine, was born. Before Madelaine was a month old, the family began calling her Sunny Jim because of a look-alike pictured on a cereal box of that era. At this time Ernest could dress himself without help, count to one hundred, spell fairly well, and sing with confidence only slightly off-key. He was a stocky lad with a quick smile and sun-bleached hair cut in Dutch-boy style.

That summer at Walloon Lake was a busy one. A second rowboat was added to the Hemingway fleet and Dr. Hemingway bought Longfield Farm, a forty-acre clearing across the lake from the cottage. While Ed Hemingway planted fruit and hardwood trees, Ernest whooped and ran about in an Indian outfit.

Many Native Americans lived in the region. Ernest often saw them picking berries or coming to Windemere to cut firewood. Ernest did not see them as romantic figures, and despite later stories, he had no special Indian friends.

Back in Oak Park, Ernest received a haircut and was sent off to first grade. Grandfather Hall had died, and Grace put the house up for sale and made plans for a larger place. Years later, Ernest recalled his mother burning household discards in the backyard of the old house. When his father's specimen jars exploded, dead snakes and other animals soared above the neighborhood.

The new house went up on a corner lot at 600 North Kenilworth Avenue. Three stories high, it had eight bedrooms, a music room where Grace could resume teaching, and an office where the doctor could receive patients.

In the summer of 1906 Ernest and a friend hitched rides to Horton Bay on horse-drawn lumber wagons to fish with Wesley Dilworth and eat trout or fried chicken at Pinehurst Cottage. But in mid-August the Hemingways returned from Walloon Lake to move into their new home. Big as it was, the house proved barely adequate. Besides the parents

Ernest, age five, often fished for trout in Horton Creek near Walloon Lake. This photo was taken in July of 1904. (Hemingway Society)

and their four children, there were now two live-in maids; and Tyley Hancock, an uncle on Grace's side of the family, began staying with them between his trips as a traveling salesman.

The music room gave Grace the chance to focus more energy on music. Ed Hemingway often cooked the meals. He was a good cook, but he did not think he should manage the servants or keep the household budget. Grace spent rashly while the doctor tried to save by preserving fruits and vegetables and keeping chickens and rabbits in the backyard. There were frequent family arguments, and Ernest usually took his father's side.

The doctor enforced the rules. No play, no games, no visits with friends were permitted on Sunday, and attendance at Sunday school and church was required. Ed Hemingway hated idleness, and Ernest and his sisters were spanked whenever they failed to do a chore.

Although Grace took Ernest to countless concerts and tried to instill an interest in the arts, Ernest preferred the many outdoor trips with his father. The doctor showed Ernest how to build a fire, cook, and make a shelter out of hemlock boughs. Ernest also learned how to dress fish and game birds for cooking. He could skin and mount small game, tie fishing flies, make bullets with a lead mold, and handle guns safely.

Ernest and Ed spent many happy afternoons walking side by side through fields, their shotguns ready for a flight of doves or jacksnipe. There was little concern at the time for conservation. Killing wild things was a respectable sport, and even in later years, Ernest never questioned this view.

Although full of energy, Ernest was awkward. Once, while running on the daily journey from Windemere to a nearby dairy for milk, he tripped with a stick in his mouth. The fall gave him a bloody gash in the back of his mouth. Fortunately his father was on hand to cauterize the wound. It was the first in scores of accidents.

In August of 1910 Grace took the eleven-year-old Ernest to Nantucket Island to visit relatives. Although he had never seen the sea before, Ernest fell in love with it at once. He swam daily, fished for sea bass and mackerel, and shipped home a swordfish's sword for the nature club's collection. The return trip included visits to revolutionary war sights in Lexington, Concord, and Boston.

His parents hoped Ernest might become a doctor, but he was beginning to show a talent for writing. In the spring of 1911 his teacher at Holmes Grammar School praised him for a story called "My First Sea Voyage." It was the first-person account of a boy from Martha's Vineyard whose sea captain father took him around Cape Horn to Australia and back aboard the three-masted schooner *Elizabeth*. Although Ernest did not admit it in school, the story was based almost entirely on his uncle Tyley Hancock's childhood experience. In adopting someone else's experience as his own, Ernest had learned a basic tool of the storyteller's art.

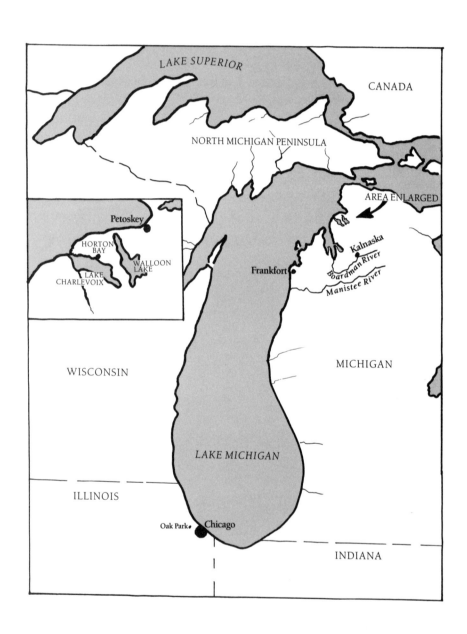

LAKE SUPERIOR

CANADA

NORTH MICHIGAN PENINSULA

AREA ENLARGED

Petoskey

HORTON
BAY

WALLOON
LAKE

LAKE
CHARLEVOIX

Kalnaska

Boardman River

Frankfort

Manistee River

WISCONSIN

MICHIGAN

LAKE MICHIGAN

ILLINOIS

Oak Park • Chicago

INDIANA

Chapter 2

The Teenager

THE SUMMER OF 1911 WAS A MEMORABLE ONE. ON JULY 19, just two days before Ernest's twelfth birthday, his sister Carol was born in the southwest bedroom of Windemere Cottage.

Uncle Willoughby and Aunt Mary Hemingway came home from Shansi Province, China, to spend the summer. Uncle Will was a missionary surgeon, and had experienced more romantic adventures than Ernest thought possible. An excellent storyteller, Uncle Will charmed the family with tales of travel in exotic lands.

Later in the summer, after Uncle Will and Aunt Mary returned to China, Ernest and his father went bird hunting in southern Illinois, where some of the doctor's cousins had farms. Once, after Ernest shot enough pigeons for a neighbor's wife to make a pie, some older boys taunted him. When one of them said he could not have shot so many birds by himself, Ernest called him a liar and was soon in a fistfight. Although he was soundly beaten, he showed no lack of courage.

That fall Ernest become a regular member of the choir at Oak Park's First Congregational Church, and in the following spring he played a minor role in *Robin Hood,* his first school play. In Michigan, the family jointly marked Carol's first and Ernest's thirteenth birthday by trimming a small hemlock tree with gifts. The birthday tree was trimmed again that fall when nineteen Hemingways gathered at the cottage to celebrate Ed Hemingways's forty-first birthday. Next, the family marked Ed and Grace's sixteenth wedding anniversary.

The most memorable event of the following summer came after a neighbor's dog tangled painfully with a porcupine. Keen for revenge, Ernest and a friend tracked and killed the porcupine. They carried it home proudly, sure that Ed Hemingway, who had spent hours cutting quills from the dog's nose, would be pleased. Instead, he angrily told the boys that wild creatures must never be killed needlessly and insisted that they cook and eat the animal rather than waste it. Although the meat was tough as leather, the two boys made a meal of it.

In the fall of 1913 Ernest entered Oak Park and River Forest Township High School, which had just been relocated in a new, four-story building. He had trouble with Latin but liked English and science. His favorite spot in the new school was the English club room. There, under a beam ceiling, Ernest discovered the excitement of literature.

He was not so happy on the playing field. At five feet four, he was one of the shortest boys in school, and much to his shame, the football coach would not let him try out for the team. He found some solace on the rifle range where, despite a weak left eye, he could outshoot most of his classmates.

Growth finally came during his fifteenth summer at Walloon Lake. Ernest and a pal camped at Longfield Farm, where they gathered hay, milked a cow, and grew enough vegetables to supply several Walloon Lake families. They delivered their produce in the family motor launch. At summer's end they harvested fifty bushels of potatoes. Although he never liked physical labor, Ernest returned to Oak Park stronger and several inches taller than when he left. He was delighted to find that he needed new clothes before he could start his sophomore year.

He still couldn't get on any football squad, however, and Grace further embarrassed him by forcing him to play the cello and take dancing lessons.

He had scores of friends and was proud of the many nicknames they gave him. He liked Porthos, after one of the Three Musketeers, was proud of Butch, and laughed at Hemingstein. Anti-Semitism was then common in the Midwest, and Ernest and his friends thought it good fun to give each other Jewish names. Hemingstein stayed with him long after he began to outgrow his prejudice.

His father gave him fifteen cents a week, and Ernest earned more by shoveling snow and delivering papers. His favorite activity, however, was long walks with the school hiking club. On the spring break of 1915 he and a friend hiked to Lake Zurich, thirty-five miles northwest of Oak Park. He returned to the happy news that a baby brother had arrived at last. Born on April 1, Leicester Clarence Hemingway, soon named the Pest, arrived too late to provide much companionship, but Ernest was proud just the same to have a brother.

At the end of their sophomore year, Ernest and a friend took the lake boat to Frankfort, Michigan, and hiked from there to Walloon Lake. The adventure took almost five days. Although they ate their fill of beans and trout, the fried chicken at Pinehurst Cottage at the end of the trip was mighty welcome.

At Windemere, the boys took down shutters and cleaned up the cabin to prepare for the arrival of the rest of the Hemingways. Then they set up their own tent camp at Longfield Farm across the lake. Dr. Hemingway, who remained most of the summer in Oak Park, had entrusted Ernest with care of the garden at Longfield and the chickens at Windemere. The doctor wrote that he was very proud of Ernest and hoped he would continue to grow in keeping with the family's Christian ideals.

Ernest, however, was beginning to stray. One day he and Sunny Jim, the tomboy of the family—and his favorite sister—scared up a blue heron while out in a boat. Although the bird was protected by game laws, Ernest impulsively shot it and left the dead bird in the boat while he and Sunny went ashore to picnic. When they returned, the bird was gone. Ernest was terrified.

Soon the game warden's son confronted Ernest with the evidence. Ernest said a stranger had given him the bird to skin and stuff. When he got home, however, he told his mother what he had done and fled. While Grace and Sunny threatened the game warden away from Windemere with a shotgun, Ernest ran all the way to his uncle George Hemingway's house at Ironton on the far side of Lake Charlevoix.

A few days later Dr. Hemingway learned of the trouble and insisted that Ernest turn himself in. The matter was settled after Ernest paid a fifteen-dollar fine, but he would recall this experience again and again with more and more embellishment. He once told a reporter that two game wardens had chased him all summer over the state of Michigan.

In his junior year at Oak Park, Ernest matured as a student. A remarkable memory helped him enjoy history. A very keen ear for language helped him finally to appreciate Latin. Thanks to continued physical growth, he at last became a substitute tackle on the lightweight football squad. He had to diet to keep under the 135-pound weight limit, and practice often left him too weary to study, but he thought it was worth it.

After the football season, his weight increased, and Ernest became a class bully. He acquired boxing gloves and insisted that his friends fight with him. Because his opponents were usually smaller than he, he almost always won. After he knocked out a much smaller friend in Grace's music room, she ordered the boys to fight outside. Although Ernest later claimed that professionals taught him to box in a Chicago gymnasium, he was mostly self-taught. He was strong enough to knock opponents out, but he lacked the speed and endurance to fight with professional boxers. It was not like Ernest, however, to admit that he had begun boxing in his mother's music room. That did not support the "tough kid" image that he soon began to build around his early years.

Ernest also enjoyed canoeing. Usually he went out with other boys, but once he took a trip on the Des Plaines River with an early girlfriend.

As his junior year progressed, he became more and more interested in writing. In English class, his themes and stories were almost always read aloud as examples for the rest of the students. A boxing story about a manager who tried and failed to fix a fight was one of his first to appear in *Tabula,* the school literary magazine. He also wrote about North Woods Indians, drawing heavily on events he had heard about or had experienced during his Michigan summers.

In addition, Ernest wrote at least one news story each issue for the *Trapeze,* the school's weekly paper. He was not a perfect speller, and the stories he pecked out on his secondhand typewriter had to be edited carefully, but he was a willing worker.

16

In the summer of 1916 Ernest became friends with Bill and Katy Smith, who were friends of the Dilworths. Bill was a twenty-year-old college student, and his sister was twenty-four, but both overlooked Ernest's youth and encouraged his company with puns and word games. They loved the Michigan woods and appreciated Ernest's outdoor knowledge and skill.

At Windemere, Ernest slept in the backyard and maintained a retreat at Murphy's Point a half mile away, where he could camp whenever he needed to be alone. He often claimed later that it was during the summer of 1916 that he lost his virginity with an Indian lass. He certainly learned little about sex from his parents. His mother would not talk about it, and his father only warned that masturbation caused blindness and that prostitutes gave men diseases.

Ernest returned for his senior year weighing 150 pounds and standing nearly six feet tall. He was still so awkward that his teammates considered him a hazard, but he became a substitute guard on the varsity football team and played enough to win his letter. He also swam for the school and was captain of what was then called the water-basketball team.

Soon after the spring thaw, Ernest and a friend paddled their canoe seventy miles down the Illinois River to Starved Rock State Park near Ottawa, Illinois. At the entrance to a canal, guards stopped them for a search. The incident reminded the boys that the United States was now at war. Like his friends, Ernest had already talked of joining the army as soon as he graduated, but his father objected. Through the influence of Uncle Tyler Hemingway, who owned a lumber business in Kansas City, Ed Hemingway had lined up a reporting job for Ernest on the *Kansas City Star*.

One weekend when Ernest and two friends camped on the Des Plaines River, they were attacked in the middle of the night by a gang of men who cut their tent ropes, threw their gear into the woods, and sent up terrifying howls. Ernest managed to throw an ax at one of the attackers before three others grabbed him and threw him into the river.

When he came up sputtering, the night was filled with laughter. The whole thing had been a hoax. The "attackers" were fellow seniors from Oak Park High. Ernest took the hoax with good humor, but years later he would tell about the night he almost killed a man with an ax. The yarn became another part of the image of the "tough kid."

Ernest poses proudly with his class plaque just before graduating from Oak Park and River Forest Township High School. (Hemingway Society)

Chapter 3

The Great Adventure

ERNEST, ONE OF 150 IN THE GRADUATING CLASS OF 1917, gave a speech as class prophet. It was a patriotic talk on America's obligation to her European allies, but his own plans did not extend much beyond another summer in Michigan.

Ed Hemingway, new owner of a Model T Ford touring car, was determined to drive it to Walloon Lake. He left Oak Park in mid-June with Grace, Leicester, and Ernest. The road was primitive. Mud holes, loose sand, and punctures delayed them often, but after six days, they chugged proudly down the grassy slope to Windemere.

The doctor arrived with big plans for Longfield Farm. With Ernest's help he moved an old house off the property, built an ice house, cut twenty acres of hay, and planted a vegetable garden. Ernest somehow found time to visit the Dilworths and the Smiths at Horton Bay. Katy and Bill had brought Carl Edgar, who was courting Katy, with them. He worked in Kansas City and lived in a small apartment, which he promised to share with Ernest.

Ernest was now impatient for the promised job to open on the *Kansas City Star*. Reporting, he believed, would improve his writing, and the job would give him an escape from his family and his father's chores.

The summer, however, had ended and the family had returned to Oak Park before Ernest was finally summoned to Kansas City. His father, who saw him to the train, said a prayer on the station platform and, with tears flowing, in front of scores of onlookers, kissed his son good-bye. Painfully embarrassed, Ernest pitied his father for the show of sentimentality.

The day after Ernest arrived in Kansas City, Uncle Tyler Hemingway took him downtown to meet his new employers. The *Star* occupied a three-story brick building that covered most of the block on Grand Avenue between Eighteenth and Twentieth streets. The unpartitioned newsroom on the second floor, lit by dusty windows and electric bulbs, was filled with rows and rows of battered desks where reporters and editors were hard at work. The clatter of typewriters made a steady din.

Ernest, offered fifteen dollars a week, was put under assistant city editor C. G. "Pete" Wellington, who trained young reporters with quiet patience and a touch of sarcasm. As soon as Ernest was shown to his desk, he sat on it and grinned with pride. Wellington recalled that he looked like a happy farm boy.

Ernest's daily beat took him to the Fifteenth Street police station for crime stories, the Union Station for interviews with noteworthy travelers, and the General Hospital for leads on accidents and crimes. He learned quickly, and his enthusiasm and energy won many friends. Wellington and several veteran reporters taught him to use the short sentences with clear, strong phrases that would one day be his trademark.

He loved to be at the center of things. Wellington recalled

that he was often hard to reach by phone because he was usually at the scene of a crime or following an ambulance to an accident. Once, when a man collapsed with a case of small-pox in Union Station, Ernest, who had been vaccinated against the disease, carried him to a cab and got him to the hospital. The doctor who handled the case became one of Ernest's best sources on raw life in the city. Ernest filed many of the doctor's stories away in memory for future use.

For a few weeks Ernest shared an apartment with Carl Edgar. It was a small, dreary place a long trolley ride from the *Star,* and Ernest soon moved to a cramped loft in an old, frame house. It was even farther from the center of town but it gave Ernest the independence he needed.

Among his many friends on the newspaper were several waiting to be called up for military service. The war dominated their conversation, and Ernest soon began talking of going to Europe himself. He did not want to miss what seemed a great adventure. His bad left eye, he knew, would keep him out of regular service, but it would not keep him from driving an ambulance. Fellow reporter Ted Brumback had already served four months in France driving an ambulance for the American Field Service and was eager to return. Ernest decided to go with him. Ed Hemingway wrote his reluctant approval, and early in January 1918 Ted and Ernest sent their applications to the Red Cross. They were told to be ready for duty in May.

They resigned from the *Star* in April and headed for Michigan for a fishing vacation. They had hardly begun fishing, however, when a telegram arrived saying they were to report at once in New York.

They reached the city in time for their physical examinations with some seventy other Red Cross volunteers on May 8. Ernest quickly began making friends with young men from all parts of America. He passed the physical easily, but the examining doctor told him that his vision was so poor he should be fitted for glasses as soon as possible. Ernest, however, would not wear glasses for several years.

While taking the two-week indoctrination course, Ernest spent his savings on a tailor-made uniform. It consisted of jodhpur breeches, a blouse with a stiff, high collar, an overseas cap, and a thirty-dollar pair of leather boots. He wore the insignia of an honorary second lieutenant and red enamel crosses on his collar and his cap. In their off hours, Ernest and Ted strolled up Broadway showing off their snappy uniforms.

On May 22, 1918, the volunteers boarded the old French liner *Chicago* and sailed for Bordeaux, France.

Two days out, a violent storm sent most men to their bunks or the ship's rail, but Ernest was only mildly ill. Near France, he was disappointed when a threatened U-boat attack did not materialize. Typhoid shots, however, proved to be as bad as expected. Everyone, including Ernest, went below with high fevers, too ill to move for several hours.

After a safe landing at Bordeaux, the volunteers rode by train to Paris, where shells from Big Bertha, the long-range German siege gun, had begun to crash. Ernest, his excitement never greater, hired a cab and took Ted on a chase through the city in search of fresh shell craters. For several hours they had no luck, but when the driver finally brought them back to their hotel, a shell screamed overhead and exploded close by with an earsplitting crash. Shrapnel from the blast knocked off a chunk of the hotel facade. Ernest went to bed fully satisfied.

Although he and most of his friends hoped to serve in France, the volunteers soon found themselves on a train bound for Italy. They arrived in Milan just hours after a huge explosion had destroyed a munitions plant. The men were put to work at once recovering human remains. They found body fragments hanging on fences and scattered across the countryside. It was Ernest's first exposure to violent death, and he was deeply moved. He recalled that his greatest shock came from finding that many of the victims were not men as he expected but women.

Two days later, after being divided into groups of twenty-five, the volunteers were sent to various sectors of the Italian front. Ernest's group, which included Ted Brumback, rode east by train to Vicenza, where ambulances carried them to Schio, a small village in the shadow of the Dolomites. The front stretched north just beyond a flank of Monte Pasubio.

The new volunteers joined American Red Cross Section Four, headquartered in an abandoned wool warehouse. The second floor was lined with two rows of army cots. The mess hall occupied the ground floor. Italian waiters served rabbit stew, pasta, wine, and the local bread, a coarse dark loaf that was suspected of containing burlap. The paved courtyard outside sheltered a fleet of twenty-three ambulances.

The Americans called their new home the Schio Country Club. Ernest soon found that the large Fiat ambulance assigned to him was difficult to maneuver up and down the steep road to the front, but more than half the driving was in daylight, and Ernest soon learned to handle the machine skillfully. The work was not as dangerous as he hoped, and because only three ambulance runs were needed on a normal day, there was much idleness.

Ernest's main pleasure was in meeting new people. There was a Red Cross canteen on the road to the front where he liked to stop and chat over a bowl of soup. One day he met

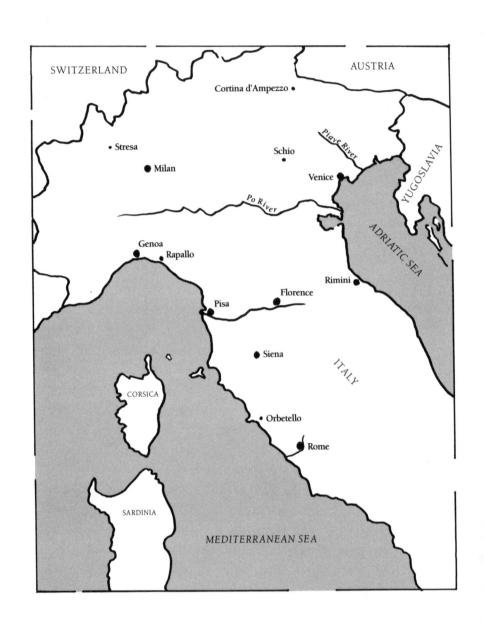

another writer from Chicago. John Dos Passos, a graduate of Harvard, had driven an ambulance in France for several months before being sent to Italy. He was three years older than Ernest, but the two men struck up a friendship that would last for many years.

When action in the mountains shifted to the Piave River valley north of Venice, some ambulances and men from Section Four were transferred there. Ernest, among those left idle at Schio, became restless and soon volunteered for canteen duty. He asked for a post close to the front. The Red Cross sent him to Fossalta, a heavily damaged village next to the flood dikes of the Piave River. The Italian army was entrenched behind the southern dikes. The Austrians held the north bank.

Although he could hear gunshots and talk to men fresh from action, Ernest was dismayed to find that the supplies needed to open his canteen had not yet arrived. He filled the hours learning Italian words and phrases and amusing the soldiers with his strange pronunciations. Even though they did not always understand him, the men enjoyed the young American's company. He ate in the officers' mess, where one of the chaplains helped him with the language and told him many stories about Italy.

When supplies finally arrived, Ernest rode his bicycle to the front lines each evening and spent the night distributing candy, cigarettes, and postcards to the men.

The evening of July 8 was a little hotter than usual, but the front when Ernest arrived seemed quieter. He parked his bike behind a command post and crept forward 150 yards to the trenches. It was very dark. He could see the Piave only when a star shell bloomed overhead and reflected on the water. Soon, the exchange of mortar and rifle picked up. Toward midnight, fighting grew intense. Above the din, Ernest heard the low whistle of an incoming mortar shell. These crude but cruel missiles were little more than canisters filled with scrap metal and black powder and armed with an impact fuse.

The shell Ernest heard struck with a white-hot explosion. It was as if a furnace door had suddenly been thrown open. The blast took his breath and pounded his ears. A splintered beam of wood struck his head and knocked him down. When his ears stopped ringing he could hear machine guns and rifles still chattering beyond the river. Nearby, a soldier sobbed in terrible pain. A second man lay deadly still.

At first Ernest could not move. He reached for the sobbing man and pulled him closer. Then, with great effort, Ernest hoisted the man on his shoulders and stood. He staggered toward the command post. A hundred yards from shelter, a bullet struck his knee. He fell. He was never able to remember how he covered the remaining distance. The Italians said that after delivering the wounded soldier to the command post, Ernest passed out.

He was carried on a stretcher to a roofless shed to await attention with scores of other wounded. So much blood drenched his tunic that he appeared to have a chest wound, but the pain was in his legs. No ambulances were immediately available, and the nearest distribution center for wounded had been evacuated because of shell fire. Ernest heard men around him die as star shells made eerie shadows on the walls. Later he said he thought of shooting himself with his pistol because death seemed more natural than life.

It was almost dawn before an ambulance took him to an emergency field station in an abandoned schoolhouse near Fornaci. It seemed to him that his legs were under the attack of a thousand hornets. A shot of morphine helped, but he had to wait several more hours before going on the operating table. Doctors removed twenty-eight shrapnel fragments from his feet and legs, but untold others were too deeply imbedded to be safely removed.

On July 17, after five days in a field hospital and two uncomfortable days on a hospital train, Ernest was delivered to the recently established American Red Cross hospital in Milan. It was in a stone mansion on a tree-lined street not far from the famous La Scala opera house. On Ernest's arrival the hospital had eighteen nurses and four patients. He was laid to bed in a private room on the top floor, overlooking the treetops.

The Italian surgeon who first examined him found no sign of infection but said that a machine gun bullet behind Ernest's right kneecap and another in his right foot must be cut out soon. While waiting for the operation, Ernest wrote to assure his parents he was in good care. Ted Brumback had already reported Ernest's heroics to Ed and Grace, but Ernest's letter, written on his nineteenth birthday, relieved them of a great deal of worry.

Ernest, at war for only six weeks, had become a genuine hero. He was the first American to be wounded in Italy. He had been recommended for the Silver Medal of Valor, Italy's highest honor.

The nurses doted on him. Within a few days Ernest knew them all and had given his favorites special names. Elsie Macdonald was "Spanish Mac," and Katherine de Long, the nurse in charge, was "Gumshoe Casey." The lovely Agnes Hannah von Kurowsky, a tall, competent brunette from Washington, D.C., soon grew very fond of Ernest. He called her "Von" and fell in love with her.

After the bullets were successfully removed from his knee and foot, Ernest began to enjoy his convalescence. He received scores of visitors. Red Cross officials came to meet the handsome young man whose exploits had been described in all the

Agnes von Kurowsky (Hemingway Society)

papers. There were also several Italians who called on the patient. Ernest glowed in the attention.

Although she did not neglect her other patients, Agnes spent much of her free time with Ernest. He wanted to marry her, but she was not ready and never let the romance go beyond the kissing stage.

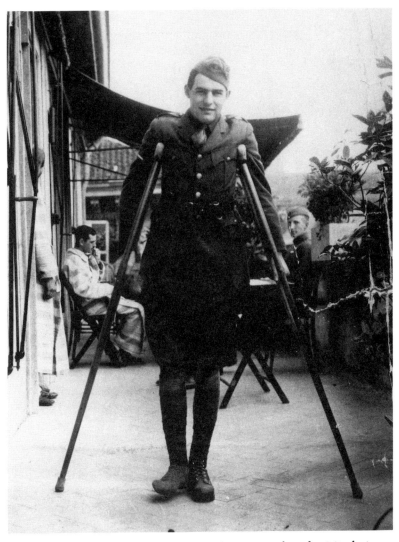

Despite crutches, Ernest exudes energy, enthusiasm, and good spirits during his convalescence in Milan. (Hemingway Society)

By mid-September, after his promotion to second lieutenant, Ernest wrote home that he would soon return to the front, maybe even join the Italian army. With the aid of a cane he could walk daily to another hospital for knee therapy. One afternoon he and two other officers escorted Elsie and Agnes and another nurse to the local racetrack, and late in September,

Ernest was about to return to the front when he squired three nurses to the racetrack. Agnes stands on his right. (Hemingway Society)

he went to Stresa on Lake Maggiore to enjoy the luxury of the Gran Hotel.

On his return to Milan, Agnes shocked him with the news that she had volunteered for duty in Florence, where there had been an outbreak of influenza. Crushed by the separation, he wrote Agnes daily, pouring out his love for her. Although she called Ernest "more precious than gold," it was clearly her hope that separation would cool his ardor.

He was still deeply in love, however, when he returned to the front. Still hobbling with a cane, he located some of his fellow volunteers on October 24 at Bassano, a few miles north of Schio. The Italians were preparing an offensive, their final big push of the war, but soon after the barrage began, Ernest fell ill with a severe case of jaundice. He barely had the strength to climb onto the return train to Milan.

Under proper care, he made a swift recovery, but the war was just about over. On November 3, while reading papers in an officers' club, he heard the news of the armistice. During the spontaneous peace celebration, Ernest met Eric "Chink" Dorman-Smith, a major in charge of British troops in Milan. The twenty-three-year-old career officer, fighting since 1914, had been wounded three times and decorated with the Military Cross for heroism. He somehow got the impression that Ernest had received his wounds while leading Italian troops in an attack on Monte Grappa and was amused a few days later when Ernest gave his true story. Dorman-Smith and Ernest became close friends, and during their frequent meetings for dinner or drinks, Ernest listened avidly to his new friend's many war stories. These tales also went into Ernest's memory for future use.

When Agnes returned from Florence in mid-November, she brought another nurse, Elsie Jessup, with her. Agnes was so often in Elsie's company that Ernest rarely had a chance to resume his courtship. And after a week in Milan, Agnes left again, this time for Treviso, near Padua, where there was another outbreak of influenza.

Ernest wanted to stay in Italy to be near Agnes, but in her letters she urged him again and again to go home. On December 9, when he visited her at Treviso, he said at last that he had decided to take her advice. He stayed in Milan long enough to celebrate Christmas with Chink Dorman-Smith, but early in January 1919 he went to Genoa and boarded a liner bound for New York.

In the spring of 1919 Ernest and his father strike a friendly pose in the back-yard of the Oak Park home. (Hemingway Society)

Chapter 4

The Hero's Return

THE RETURN TO CIVILIAN LIFE WAS DIFFICULT FOR the nineteen-year-old Hemingway. As everybody's hero, his triumphant homecoming only delayed the inevitable adjustment. He loved the attention and wanted to prolong it.

Before getting off the ship, Ernest, with a cane, and a black cape over his uniform, told a reporter from the *New York Sun* that he had taken part in the heavy fighting on Monte Grappa. Ernest showed no embarrassment when the paper printed the lie.

In Oak Park, Ernest was touched by his father's tears of joy and glowed in the warm reception from the rest of his family and his friends.

A reporter from the *Oak Parker* found Ernest reluctant to talk about himself and shy about being a hero but willing to do it all again if necessary. Ernest thrilled two eleven-year-old girls in the neighborhood by showing them his war souvenirs. He shot off a star shell in the backyard for them and told them endless war stories.

He was asked to speak to several groups, including a student assembly at his old high school. He described his battle experience in graphic detail and showed souvenirs, including the shredded, bloodstained breeches he was wearing the night he was wounded. His talk was a great hit.

It did not take Ernest long, however, to feel the pinch of family restrictions. His parents still thought of him as a child and were shocked to discover that he enjoyed smoking and drinking.

Ernest was lonely for his old pals, many of whom had not yet come home. And he was still in love with Agnes. Her letters made him wish he had stayed in Italy. He wrote her almost daily until March, when she sent the devastating news that she had fallen in love and was about to marry an Italian lieutenant from Naples.

Ernest went to bed with a fever. He wrote Elsie Macdonald in a rage, describing Agnes's treachery and wishing her ill luck. Later, with his temperature back to normal and some pride restored, he boasted to friends that several other women had helped him forget Agnes. In April and May he actually did have a few dates with a local girl who enjoyed canoeing and listened to Ernest read the short stories he was beginning to write. When Ernest gave her his black cape, however, an angry Grace demanded its return. This cooled the romance and made Ernest more anxious than ever to leave home.

Writing eased his frustrations. Although his stories were certainly better than his high school efforts, he tried to cram too much into each one. His descriptions were too wordy. His dialogue did not advance the narrative.

He went to Michigan in June several days ahead of his family and spent most of his free time at Horton Bay with Bill Smith. Ernest planted vegetables, tended apple trees, fished, and did some serious smoking and drinking.

When a letter came from Agnes saying her romance with

the Neapolitan lieutenant had ended and she was thinking of coming home, Ernest did not respond. His wounded pride would not let him revive the affair.

Although his wounds continued to fester, and pieces of metal still had to be removed from time to time, his legs were strong enough by July to take a fishing trip with Bill Smith. Traveling in Bill's old Buick, they spent five days in the pine barrens southeast of Horton Bay. They saw deer, flushed many flocks of partridge, and even scared up a bear. Fishing was great. On their final day they caught sixty-four trout between them.

When they returned, Ed Hemingway enlisted Ernest's help in building a cabin on Longfield Farm that Grace could use for a studio. Ernest wrote in his spare time and received encouragement from Edwin Balmer, a novelist who was spending the summer at Walloon Lake. Balmer gave Ernest the names of several magazine editors who might want his stories. Ernest sold nothing, but Balmer's interest gave him fresh confidence.

On a second trip to the pine barrens, Ernest and Bill Smith took two friends with them. Good weather, good fishing, and good company put them in such high spirits that on the way home they shot out a half dozen streetlights while speeding through Boyne City. The episode supported Ernest's tough image and gave some small truth to his later claim that he spent his youth shooting up the small towns of Michigan.

Later in the summer he and two friends spent a week fishing in Michigan's Upper Peninsula. This experience would later inspire "Big Two-Hearted River," in which the hero, Nick Adams, takes a solo fishing trip trying to recover from the physical and mental wounds of war.

Ernest went to Horton Bay often to see Marjorie Bump, seventeen, a waitress at the Dilworths' Pinehurst Cottage. They rowed onto the lake after dark and often landed on an isolated beach to build a fire and eat a picnic supper. In September, when Marjorie returned to high school, Ernest began taking long evening walks with another, older waitress. One evening perhaps ended with a sexual encounter on the end of the Dilworth dock. The experience, real or imagined, inspired him to write "Up in Michigan," a short story with such a graphic sex scene that it remained unpublished in the United States for years.

Ernest extended his stay with the Dilworths well into the fall to help them harvest potatoes, and when he returned to Oak Park in October it was only to tell his family he had decided to winter in Petoskey, where he hoped to find the solitude he needed to write.

Once installed in a second-story bedroom in a boarding house on Petoskey's State Street, Ernest did write diligently. Day after day, he pecked at his portable typewriter through the morning and well into the afternoon. When high school let out, however, he usually went out to meet Marjorie Bump and walk her home, and he found time for other friends. Once, during an evening party in a cabin, Ernest held several young men and women spellbound with his war stories. Later he gave a speech much like his earlier high school talk to the Ladies' Aid Society in the Petoskey Public Library.

Among those impressed by the talk was Harriet Gridley Connable from Toronto, Canada. Her husband headed the Canadian branch of the F. W. Woolworth stores. Their son, Ralph, Jr., a year younger than Ernest, had been lame from birth. Mrs. Connable invited Ernest to be a paid companion for the boy while the parents went to Palm Beach for a few months. The Connable mansion was fully staffed with servants. The boys could go to concerts, hockey games, and boxing matches. Ernest promised to be in Toronto soon after the holidays.

Ernest found the Connables generous and friendly. When he expressed interest in a job with the *Toronto Star,* Mr. Connable took him downtown at once to meet one of the paper's executives. Ernest toured the building and had a friendly chat with features editor Greg Clark.

The *Star* published both a daily and a weekly. Clark, who worked for the weekly, was impressed when the young visitor said he had once worked for the highly regarded *Kansas City Star.* And when Ernest said he wanted a job, Clark introduced him to J. H. Cranston, editor of the weekly. Cranston said he could pay Ernest almost a penny a word for feature stories. Ernest went to work, and by mid-May his stories began appearing under his byline.

He played two roles with different costumes for each. At the Connables he dressed like a college boy in sweater and slacks. He followed all the rules of polite society. At the newspaper office he wore a scruffed leather jacket over a faded red shirt. He spoke out of the side of his mouth in short, broken phrases. He stood on the balls of his feet like a boxer about to throw a punch. He told Cranston he had been a tough kid and had spent his youth riding freight trains and living in hobo camps.

Ernest sent samples of recent fiction to Edwin Balmer, who replied that some of his stories would sell, if not now, maybe later. This proved to be fairly accurate. Literary tastes would change before Ernest's stories saw print.

While the Connables were away, Ernest wrote almost every day. In the evenings, he took young Ralph to hockey games and boxing matches. When the parents returned, John Bone, managing editor for the *Star* daily, offered Ernest a full-time job, but he was eager to see Michigan again and turned down the offer with thanks.

He soon regretted the decision. His parents, still treating him like a boy, made life miserable at Walloon Lake. He turned petulant under Grace's constant scolding. He grumbled over some chores and refused to do others. Tempers grew raw.

The blowup came after a secret all-night picnic that included the Hemingway girls and some girls from a neighboring cottage. The girls, taking Ernest with them, snuck out after the adults were asleep and spent most of the night on a remote beach. Their absence was discovered, however, and when they returned at three A.M. the worried parents of both households were waiting for them. An irate Grace falsely accused Ernest of planning the escapade and ordered him to leave Windemere. His father, more sad than angry, said he would continue to pray for Ernest.

He went on a six-day fishing trip with friends but complained most of the time about being an "orphan." For the first time he began speaking bitterly of his mother. When Grace learned she had been wrong about Ernest's part in the picnic, she tried to make amends by inviting Ernest to Windemere for lunch. He did not show up.

After the family returned to Oak Park, Ernest stayed at Horton Bay with Bill Smith's brother, Kenley, and his wife, Doodles. When they offered to share their Chicago apartment with him, Ernest quickly accepted. It proved to be a lucky decision.

Chapter 5

Hadley

IN 1910, AFTER ELIZABETH HADLEY RICHARDSON graduated from a private girls' school in her native St. Louis, she attended college for just one year before coming home to care for her widowed mother, an invalid.

Although she was a tall, pretty woman with auburn hair and quiet manners, Hadley was now twenty-eight, and caring for her mother had kept her confined so long she was beginning to think of herself as a spinster. When her mother finally died, Hadley was exhausted and emotionally drained. An invitation from Katy Smith to visit Chicago was a chance to recover her spirits and return to a world she had almost forgotten.

Hadley discovered that Katy, a friend since high school, was one of several young people sharing Kenley and Doodles Smith's apartment. The redhead from St. Louis was introduced to a confusing collection of guests, including a bulky six-footer who seemed to dominate the household with his energy and enthusiasm.

To add to the confusion, everyone spoke a jargon that sometimes sounded like a foreign language. Money was "seed." Cigarettes were "pills." A joke was "laughage," food "eatage," and death "mortgage." Everyone went by several names. The big leader's names included "Oinbones," "Hemmy," and "Hemingstein." Hadley won Ernest's admiration when she said she was known at home as "Hash," but he was more impressed by Hadley's confident manner and skill at the piano.

When she returned to St. Louis, she and Ernest began to exchange letters. He told about his writing, his money worries, and his various jobs. For a time he wrote advertising copy for a tire company. Later he put out a monthly magazine for the Cooperative Society of America, which paid him forty dollars a week.

In March, after Hadley wrote that she loved him and wanted to love him even more, Ernest bought a new suit and went to St. Louis by train for a weekend visit. Two weeks later Hadley visited Chicago again. Thanks to Ernest's influence, the entire Smith household by now was caught up in boxing and writing.

Hadley and Ernest talked seriously about their future. She was older by eight years and worried about their age difference. He wanted to return to Italy before settling down. Hadley was getting three thousand dollars a year from a family trust fund, enough at the time for a couple to live modestly in Europe.

Kenley Smith had introduced Ernest to Sherwood Anderson, whose latest book, *Winesburg, Ohio,* had established him as the leading writer of his era. Anderson urged Ernest and Hadley to settle in Paris, where scores of expatriate artists and writers were doing exciting work.

By May, Ernest and Hadley had agreed to get married, but they did not know when or where they would live. Grace, convinced that marriage would improve Ernest, encouraged them and sent Hadley a warm letter, offering Windemere Cottage as a honeymoon retreat.

Grace and Leicester join the newlyweds for a wedding picture taken in the Dilworths' garden soon after the services. (Hemingway Society)

Finally, on September 3, 1921, in a Protestant church in Horton Bay, Ernest and Hadley exchanged wedding vows. It was a hot day, and because of his wounds, Ernest had difficulty kneeling, but the service was soon over, and the party adjourned to Pinehurst Cottage, where Liz Dilworth put on a wedding feast. From there the newlyweds escaped to Windemere Cottage for two weeks of solitude.

They had planned to live with Kenley and Doodles, but Ernest had made the mistake of repeating a Smith family confidence to an outsider. Kenley was so angry when he heard about it that he withdrew his hospitality. Hadley and Ernest thus began married life in a drab, top-floor apartment in the

1300 block of North Clark Street. Ernest had given up his magazine job, and although he wrote a few articles for Cranston in Toronto, they lived mostly on Hadley's annuity.

Anderson kept raving about Paris and promised to give the Hemingways letters of introduction to Gertrude Stein, who held a Saturday night salon for intellectuals, Sylvia Beach, who ran the Shakespeare and Company bookstore, and many others.

By November, Ernest and Hadley were convinced. They took the train for New York and boarded a steamship bound for France.

Paris was everything Anderson had promised. Lewis Galantière, a friend of Anderson's, was among the first to greet them. A clever mimic, Galantière made Hadley laugh so hard during their first evening together that she could hardly eat. Back in their temporary hotel room, Ernest persuaded Galantière to spar with him. It was a one-sided contest. Outweighed and with little experience, Galantière took off his gloves and put on his glasses after the first round. Ernest, however, continued to throw playful punches and knocked Galantière's glasses to the floor, where they shattered.

Ernest's apologies and natural charm saved the friendship, and soon after the first of the year, Galantière helped the Hemingways find an apartment in a cheap but squalid part of the Latin Quarter. The fourth-floor apartment came with large, ugly furniture. Each floor had a single toilet located on the stairway landing. Noise thundered nightly from a workmen's dance hall next door, and around the corner, drunks and prostitutes had given Café des Amateurs a bad name.

Hadley and Ernest, however, were delighted to have their own home at last. He wrote every morning, trying now to base his stories on experience. His earlier efforts, he decided, were too inventive to be convincing. Instead of pecking at a type-writer, he wrote in longhand, filling notebooks with first drafts. Whether working on a poem or a short story, he strove for a more simple, more direct style and began talking about the "true sentence." He eliminated whatever seemed elaborate or wordy. Often he would cross out sentence after sentence, de-stroying the work of an entire morning. When he got a sentence he liked, however, he would build on it.

When noises in the apartment building began distracting him, he rented a bedroom in a nearby hotel for his office, and despite the cold, he worked there every morning. In the after-noons he often walked the paths of the Luxembourg Gardens. In the museums he admired paintings by Cézanne and Monet. He wanted to achieve with writing what these artists achieved with paint. When out of his office, he tried not to think about writing. This, he believed, allowed his subconscious to take over. Next day, when the words flowed, he was convinced that the discipline worked.

At first Ernest thought of most of the other expatriates in Paris as loafers posing as intellectuals. He was introduced to Ezra Pound, who was so full of literary opinions that Ernest felt sure he was just another poseur. A few days later, however, after Pound said he liked some of Ernest's poems and asked for boxing lessons, Ernest's opinion changed.

Gertrude Stein won Ernest's respect at once. He was fas-cinated by her forceful personality. She was stimulating. She made everything seem important. She read some of his work and said his descriptive passages were not particularly good. Ernest's respect grew. He had already arrived at the same opin-ion. She liked his poems, and although she thought the short story "Up in Michigan" was well written, she told him it was unsalable because of the explicit sex.

Gertrude had literary prejudices. She did not like James Joyce and would not at first discuss Sherwood Anderson's work. Later, Ernest met Joyce and admired both the man and his work.

Ernest also spent many happy afternoons with Sylvia Beach in her bookstore and lending library. All writers were welcome there, and Ernest later recalled that no other person in Paris was kinder to him than Sylvia.

Through weekly meetings of the Anglo-American Press Club, Ernest met Guy Hickok, a correspondent for the *Brooklyn Daily Eagle* who shared Ernest's interest in sports. Hickok, a veteran journalist, gave Ernest much useful advice, and Hadley and Guy's wife, Mary, became close friends.

After meeting Hickok, Ernest began sending two articles a week to the *Toronto Star*. Editor John Bone was pleased and asked Ernest to cover the 1922 international economic conference in Genoa, Italy, in April. Ernest found events outside the conference there more interesting than the meetings and the diplomats.

One day he and Bill Bird, correspondent for the Consolidated Press, inspected Genoa's slums. Ernest described them as one of the breeding grounds of Italian communism. In all, Ernest sent Bone fifteen reports on the Genoa trip, and when he returned to Paris, he and Hadley had enough money for a vacation.

They asked Chink Dorman-Smith, then stationed in Germany, to join them at Chamby, Switzerland, not far from the eastern shore of the Lake of Geneva. There, Ernest and Chink resumed their long evenings of good-natured debate. Once they got into a beer-drinking contest at a local café. When they staggered back to the hotel, arm in arm, they woke the village with their singing.

At the end of May, they decided to hike into Italy. Hadley did not have proper boots for the snow, and by the time they reached the 8,110-foot-high pass of St. Bernard, her shoes were falling apart. The well-booted Chink and Ernest ended the trip practically carrying Hadley between them. When they reached the train station at Aosta, she was in agony and slept all the way to Milan.

Chink returned to his regiment. Hadley nursed her blisters, and Ernest interviewed Benito Mussolini, head of the Fascist party, which was about to take control of Italy. Ernest was impressed and sent a hopeful report to readers in Toronto. Mussolini seemed to have the strength and intelligence, Ernest wrote, to cure Italy's postwar woes. Later, however, he changed his mind and saw Mussolini and fascism as evil forces.

Ernest took Hadley to Schio and was disappointed. The town seemed smaller and dirtier than Ernest remembered it from 1918. The Schio Country Club, a wool mill again, was polluting the stream where he and fellow volunteers once swam. The inn was so uncomfortable that they left after one sleepless night.

They went next to Fossalta in a rented car to search for the spot where Ernest had been wounded. The town had been rebuilt with cheap houses, and the trenches on the south bank of the Piave River had been filled in and smoothed over.

Back in Paris, they found the June heat oppressive. They had spent all their savings. There were no new assignments from John Bone. Ernest was not sure he could get his writing started again.

Chapter 6

Changing Fortunes

BY STARTING EARLY WHILE THE NEIGHBORHOOD WAS still cool and quiet, Ernest found he was able to write. Visitors, however, distracted him.

He enjoyed seeing John Dos Passos, who had by now written two books, including *Three Soldiers*, a powerful antiwar novel. Dos Passos stayed with the Hemingways only long enough to have an evening meal with them; many other visitors stayed longer.

The heat grew worse, and in August, Ernest and Hadley escaped with two other couples to Germany's Black Forest. They hiked and fished until Ernest tripped over a log and took to bed for a day with an injured back.

From the Black Forest, Ernest and Hadley went on by themselves to Cologne, where Chink Dorman-Smith was stationed with the British army of occupation. Angry citizens, protesting postwar inflation, had recently killed a Cologne policeman. Ernest described the unrest in a dispatch for the *Toronto Star*, and when the Hemingways returned to Paris, there was a cable from John Bone waiting for him. He liked the Cologne article and wanted Ernest to hurry to Constan-

tinople (now Istanbul) and cover final battles of the war between the Turks and the Greeks.

Hadley protested that the assignment was too dangerous,
and when Ernest insisted on going anyway, she stopped speaking to him. He left without saying good-bye. Meanwhile, Ernest
had secretly agreed to cover the war for the International News
Service as well as the *Star*. This violated his exclusive agreement
with Bone, but Ernest needed the extra money.

He arrived in Constantinople on September 29, 1922. It
was a difficult war to cover. The Greeks wanted to censor
dispatches so heavily that most newsmen went to British
sources. The British had recently intervened to protect the
Dardanelles from the advancing Turks. Meanwhile, Greek refugees had begun to flee from Constantinople.

Not suspecting that they were written by the same man,
Bone complained that Ernest's reports duplicated the International News Service dispatches. Ernest was too sick to care.
He had contracted malaria and could not leave his hotel room
for several days.

While he was ill, the warring armies came to terms of a
sort. Some Greek territory in eastern Thrace was ceded to the
Turks, and the Greek army was given three days to evacuate.
Despite chills and fever, Ernest covered the desperate retreat
as best he could. He arrived in Adrianople on October 17 to
find the only hotel full. He slept in the hotel office and woke
covered with lice. That day he joined some American photog-
raphers to watch silent columns of Greek refugees fleeing their
homeland. The tragic scene haunted him long after he returned
to Paris.

Hadley, who had forgiven him fully, nursed Ernest back
to health. His three weeks on assignment had earned four
hundred dollars, enough, Ernest decided, to let him focus on

poetry and short stories for several weeks. Fresh incentive came when Ezra Pound asked Ernest to contribute to one of six small books by contemporary writers that Pound planned to publish. The books would be printed by Ernest's fellow journalist, Bill Bird, who had just bought a printing press. With Pound's offer in mind, Ernest wrote "My Old Man," a story about a boy who discovers that his jockey father is a crook.

Meanwhile, Ernest was delighted to find a sparring partner in Henry "Mike" Strater, an American artist who painted several portraits of Ernest during their long friendship. The first, painted right after a sparring session, shows Ernest looking down thoughtfully, as if he were resting between rounds.

Late in November Bone asked Ernest to cover the diplomatic settlement of the Turkish-Greek dispute, in Lausanne, Switzerland. While there, he showed "My Old Man" to Lincoln Steffens, a veteran reporter Ernest had met on earlier assignments. Steffens liked it so much he tried to sell it to *Cosmopolitan* for Ernest. Although the effort failed, Steffens's enthusiasm was encouraging.

He was in high spirits when he went to the train station to meet Hadley, who was coming to Switzerland to spend the holidays with him. He was shocked to find her in tears. Her sobs were so heavy that it took Ernest several minutes to learn the trouble. All his manuscripts, originals, carbons, and notebooks, Hadley finally blurted out, had been stolen at the Paris train station. She had packed them in a valise to bring as a surprise for Ernest so he could work over the holidays, but while her luggage was being loaded on the train, the valise disappeared.

Ernest did his best to calm her. He could not believe, however, that she had packed the carbons as well as the originals. He took the next train back to Paris and searched the apartment before he was convinced of the truth.

The loss drained his confidence. When the Lausanne conference ended and he and Hadley took a skiing vacation in the Swiss Alps, he was in a dark mood. He was still depressed when they arrived in Rapallo, Italy, where Dorothy and Ezra Pound had recently established a second home. Mike Strater, also visiting the Pounds, had sprained an ankle and could not box. Ernest hoped to tell his trouble to Ezra, but the poet abruptly went away without saying when he would return.

It was at this time that Hadley announced that she was pregnant. Ernest was both pleased and worried. Could they afford a child? He tried to write, but had little luck. Later, he would tell friends that the loss of his early work was probably a good thing, but during the first few days at Rapallo it seemed an insurmountable disaster.

Two visiting publishers helped bring him out of his gloom. Edward O'Brien, who published a literary journal in Paris, wanted to use "My Old Man" in his next collection of short stories, and Robert McAlmon who had just launched a publishing firm for expatriate authors, asked to see some of Ernest's work.

When Ezra returned with plans for an ambitious walking tour, Ernest's spirits were much improved, and the tour proved a great success. The Pounds and the Hemingways, all with light packs, picnicked at midday and took their evening meals at the country inns where they stopped for the night. They hiked through Pisa and Siena and continued south as far as Orbetello. Ezra, who knew the history of the region well, was an excellent guide, but when they came to a battleground, Ernest took over, surprising Ezra with his knowledge of military history and strategy.

At the end of the walk, the Pounds returned to Rapallo while Ernest and Hadley headed for the mountains north of Venice to stay at the small town of Cortina d'Ampezzo. There

Ernest was able to write again. He worked on miniatures: short, precise paragraphs describing events he had either heard about or experienced. There was one on the Greek refugees at Adrianople (Edirne) and another on a bullfight based on descriptions from Mike Strater and Gertrude Stein. He skied every afternoon. Hadley meanwhile befriended the pianist Renata Borgatti, who shared her love for walking.

When John Bone cabled asking Ernest to go to the Ruhr Valley, Ernest left Hadley with Renata and went on assignment again. He filed ten dispatches from the Ruhr, describing the growing tension over France's occupation of what had once been German territory. His articles, based on interviews with politicians and ordinary citizens, are among his best journalistic work.

Soon after returning to Cortina, he wrote his first short story since the loss of his manuscripts. "Out of Season," a great improvement over earlier work, tells of a drunken guide in a mountain village who tries to persuade a young tourist to fish the trout streams out of season. This parallels the marital tensions growing between the young man and his wife. The two themes reinforce each other and give the story great emotional impact. In future work, Ernest would use the technique skillfully again and again.

He was still restless for travel when he and Hadley returned to Paris in May of 1923. He wanted to go to Spain and see some bullfights. He persuaded Bill Bird and Robert McAlmon to go with him. McAlmon, who had married a wealthy woman, agreed to pay the way. Bird's job with Consolidated Press restricted his vacation time, but he agreed to meet Ernest and Robert in Madrid as soon as he could.

Once in Spain, Ernest became a bullfight fan almost overnight. Although he had seen just a few minor fights when Bird arrived, Ernest already knew all the bullfighting terms and spoke as if he had grown up with the sport. He talked endlessly about courage. McAlmon saw bullfighting as a cruel sport. He reacted with horror when he first saw a bull disembowel a horse.

In Seville, Bird and McAlmon preferred watching the café dancers rather than the bulls, but Ernest insisted that they continue to Ronda to see more bullfights. There he showed so much enthusiasm for the sport, McAlmon suspected it was a pose. There was a great deal of tension among the three friends when the trip ended, but soon after returning to Paris, McAlmon announced plans to publish a volume of Ernest's short stories and poems.

Ernest, however, could talk of little more than an early return to Spain. Gertrude Stein recommended the week-long Festival of San Fermín held in Pamplona every July. This time, he took Hadley with him. They were both charmed by Pamplona, a Basque town in the highlands of northern Spain.

The festival, which began July 6, attracted all the best matadors of Spain. Fireworks lit the night sky. There was music, dancing, and much drinking. Churches held special masses. Each morning the bulls, taunted by amateurs and cheered on by spectators, ran a mile and a half through the city streets to the Plaza de Toros. Each afternoon, with trumpets blaring, the professionals entered the ring. In five days, the Hemingways saw five men gored.

Unfortunately, before their stay ended, Hadley caught a bad cold. It grew worse on their return to Paris. Ernest became so concerned, he could not write. When she began to recover, they made plans to sail for Canada, where Hadley would have her baby and Ernest would work for the *Toronto Star*. A distracted Ernest could write no more than two or three hours a day.

McAlmon, meanwhile, asked for twelve more of Ernest's

miniatures for the forthcoming book. He wrote five on bull-fighting and seven based on various reporting assignments. McAlmon quickly set the book in type and delivered the galleys to Ernest.

His main disappointment with *Three Stories and Ten Poems* was that it would be a very thin volume. Gertrude Stein suggested that a table of contents and some blank front pages be added to beef up the book. When he returned the proofs, Ernest relayed the idea to McAlmon. Then the Hemingways sailed for home. It was August 15, 1923.

Chapter 7

In Our Time

MANY FRIENDS, INCLUDING GREG CLARK, AN OLD friend from the *Star*, welcomed the Hemingways in Toronto. While Clark's wife, Helen, helped Hadley find an apartment, Ernest reported to the *Toronto Star* and found that his friend John Bone had been promoted. Harry Hindmarsh had replaced him as city editor.

Hindmarsh, thinking Ernest was too cocky, proceeded to make his life uncomfortable. Ernest drew out-of-town assignments repeatedly, and even though the baby was due in October, Hindmarsh sent Ernest to New York at that time to cover the visit of British prime minister David Lloyd George. Ernest filed six reports on Lloyd George and hurried home, failing to cover a welcoming ceremony where the deputy mayor of New York made news by criticizing British policy.

On October 10, as soon as his train reached Toronto, Ernest rushed to the hospital, arriving soon after the baby. John Hadley Nicanor Hemingway weighed seven pounds, five ounces. The parents included Nicanor to honor one of their favorite Pamplona matadors. The baby, however, was soon known as Bumby, a nickname that would stick with him into his adult life.

After Hindmarsh berated Ernest for missing the critical speech in New York and for going to the hospital before reporting to the office, the editor demoted him to writing features for the weekly edition of the *Star*. That night Ernest and Hadley agreed to return to Paris as soon as Bumby was old enough to travel.

When the first copies of *Three Stories and Ten Poems* arrived in Toronto, Ernest expected reviews to follow, but none appeared. He was keenly disappointed. On top of this, he learned that just 170 instead of the expected 300 copies of the Ezra Pound book had been published. And *in our time,* as it was called, was also ignored by the critics.

After a brief visit in Oak Park with Hadley and the baby, Ernest returned to Toronto and resigned from the *Star*. The Hemingways soon took the train to New York, and on January 19, 1924, they sailed for France. They found a more comfortable apartment not far from the Luxembourg Gardens and within easy walking distance of Gertrude Stein's. It was a respectable neighborhood with a pleasant café nearby. The main drawback was a noisy lumberyard and sawmill right below their windows. The throb of the mill's old engine and the scream of the saw often drove Ernest to the café to do his writing.

Ezra Pound persuaded Ernest to take a part-time, nonpaying job with English novelist Ford Madox Ford, who had just launched the *transatlantic review*, a monthly literary magazine. The work cut into his writing time and he thought Ford was a literary snob, but Ernest enjoyed reading the manuscripts submitted for the magazine. He thought it was instructive, and sometimes, as an exercise, he rewrote a story, trying to make it better. Every Thursday, Ford gave literary teas in the *review* office, and at one of them Ernest met Harold Loeb, founder

Ernest strikes a confident pose in the courtyard of his 1924 Paris home. (Special Collections and Archives, Knox College Library, Galesburg, Illinois)

of *Broom,* another literary magazine. Ernest and Hadley soon became friends with Loeb and his friend Kitty Cannell. Both Kitty and Harold, however, were wealthy, while Ernest and Hadley were poor. The difference caused problems. Ernest resented it when Kitty took Hadley shopping and bought clothes for her that Ernest could not afford. This happened at a time when Hadley's trust, which had been badly managed, was yielding less each month and when Ernest was no longer receiving money from the *Star*.

His friendship with Gertrude Stein improved when he persuaded Ford to start serializing her long, yet unpublished novel, *The Making of Americans,* in the *review*. The installments began in April, and Gertrude was thrilled. The April issue also carried a Hemingway story and, at last, some favorable reviews of his two books.

His writing day continued to begin early. He boiled bottles, made baby formula, and gave Bumby his first bottle. Then, while the neighborhood was still quiet, he wrote at the dining room table. When the sawmill started, he usually went to a café to continue writing.

Some stories were set in Paris, but most of them drew on his experiences in the Michigan woods. "Indian Camp," which appeared in the April *review*, tells of a doctor and his son called out in the middle of the night for a cesarean delivery in an Indian shack. Despite the crude surroundings, the baby arrives safely, but the doctor and his son discover that the woman's husband, driven mad by her screams, has cut his throat from ear to ear. Although the death-birth contrast gives impact, the story's main strength comes from the relationship between the doctor and Nick Adams, his young son. He wrote several other Nick Adams stories at this time, including the long "Big Two-Hearted River," based on his 1919 fishing trip in Michigan's Upper Peninsula.

When not writing, Ernest might go to a gymnasium where he could usually find a sparring partner, help a waiter he knew tend a vegetable garden, or play tennis with Harold Loeb or Ezra Pound. Sometimes he spent an entire afternoon in Sylvia

Beach's bookstore and lending library. Thanks to complimen-tary tickets from his newspaper friends, he could see prizefights whenever he wished and for a time was a fan of both the indoor and outdoor bicycle races. In the evenings, Ernest and Hadley often left the baby with the maid to have dinner with friends.

His relationship with Ford, never friendly, worsened in the summer of 1924. Ford went traveling, leaving Ernest in charge of two issues. In one, he printed a satirical review Ford never would have allowed, and he loaded the next with work by American authors. When Ford returned, he printed an apology for what had happened in his absence. Ernest was irate.

Meanwhile, he and Hadley, along with Chink Dorman-Smith, John Dos Passos, Robert McAlmon, Bill and Sally Bird, the writer Donald Ogden Stewart, and several other friends went to Pamplona to see the bulls. Ernest impressed his friends every morning by taking part in the amateur corrida. Although the bull's horns were padded, the animal could knock a man down and cause serious bruises. It took courage to join the amateurs. Stewart, the only other member of the party to face the bulls with Ernest, suffered cracked ribs when tossed by an angry bull.

After the festival, Ernest led his delegation trout fishing north of town. Next day, while some of the group began hiking over the Pyrenees into France, Hadley and Ernest returned to Paris by train.

When he learned that the *transatlantic review* was about to fold for lack of funds, Ernest persuaded Krebs Friend, whom he had first met in Chicago, to come to the rescue. Friend, who had a wealthy wife, put up two hundred dollars a month for six months to keep Ford in business.

Meanwhile, Donald Stewart, John Dos Passos, and Harold Loeb had all been urging Ernest to find an American publisher who would bring out his stories in one volume. Loeb, whose own book had just been accepted by the publisher Horace Liveright, introduced Ernest to Liveright's literary scout. The man was Jewish, however, and Ernest, still full of prejudice, refused to show him any work. Loeb, also Jewish, was shocked and dismayed, but he continued to give Ernest his friendship and support.

Loeb's companion, Kitty Cannell, had discovered that Ernest, charming as he might be, gossiped maliciously and often said the meanest things about those who had helped him most. The main purpose of some Hemingway stories at this time seemed to be to ridicule and satirize friends. Kitty wondered how Ernest's circle of friends continued to expand.

It was at this time he began a long and happy friendship with the American poet Archibald MacLeish. He also befriended Ernest Walsh, who was about to launch *This Quarter,* another literary magazine. Walsh purchased "Big Two-Hearted River" for publication, paying more than Ernest had received for both of his books.

The influential American critic Edmund Wilson had finally praised both *in our time* and *Three Stories and Ten Poems* for their clean prose style. Ernest hoped the reviews might interest a publisher in his collection of new stories, but nothing happened. His money worries grew worse. When a friend described Schruns, a resort town in the Austrian Alps where inflation was steadily improving the value of American dollars, Ernest and Hadley decided to sublet their apartment and try saving money in Austria. Schruns was all they hoped. The Hemingways could actually come out a little ahead each month. He was able to write, and the skiing was excellent.

They took rooms on the second floor of a local hotel. There was a single-lane bowling alley for Ernest and a piano for Hadley. Because skiing had not yet become popular, they had the slopes to themselves. After finding a maid to care for Bumby, they soon began making friends among the villagers. Ernest became a regular at the hotel poker table. He feared at first that writing would be impossible without the stimulus of a big city, but after a struggle, he began working on stories again. Don Stewart sent a personal check to boost Ernest's morale. Loeb wrote saying he planned to show some of Ernest's stories to New York publishers.

In mid-January, when heavy snows began, a local ski instructor led the Hemingways and a few others into the high country for some quality skiing. They spent their first night in a rustic inn. Next morning, wearing heavy packs and with sealskins on their skis, they continued to climb. As porters carried their supplies to an Alpine shelter at the crest of a ridge, Ernest spotted deer, chamois, ptarmigan, foxes, and martins. Ernest was thrilled by the time he topped a high ridge and looked down on a field of virgin snow. After skiing until the light failed, they entered the shelter and fell into an exhausted sleep on the bunks.

Ernest could not get his fill of the high-country skiing. They went up again in February. It was a memorable trip. After taking top money in the evening poker game, Ernest skied down the face of a glacier next day at speeds he never thought possible. That night great news arrived from New York. Horace Liveright wanted to bring out an American edition of *In Our Time*—this time with capital letters.

Chapter 8

The Novelist

ALTHOUGH ERNEST HAD FOUND IT DIFFICULT TO write in Austria, the news from Liveright put him to work. The publisher wanted a substitute for the sexually explicit "Up in Michigan." Ernest had a story in rough draft about a punch-drunk ex-boxer who, despite former fame, is barely surviving as a hobo. Ernest pecked out a final version on a borrowed typewriter and mailed the story to New York.

Later he wrote an article praising Ezra Pound for the first issue of Ernest Walsh's *This Quarter,* and as soon as the Hemingways returned to Paris, they helped put the issue together. Hadley read proof while Ernest collected photos and edited articles. Although they were not paid for this work, Walsh bought "The Undefeated," one of Ernest's first bullfighting stories, for a later issue of the magazine.

Marital problems began for the Hemingways when Harold Loeb and Kitty Cannell introduced them to the Pfeiffer sisters. Pauline and Virginia grew up in Arkansas and attended a Catholic convent in St. Louis not far from Hadley's childhood home. The elder, Pauline, a recent graduate of the University of Missouri, was editor of the Paris edition of *Vogue* magazine and in the market for a husband.

Pauline claimed later that she was not at first interested in Ernest but felt sorry for Hadley because of her secondhand clothes and cheap apartment. Her friendship with Hadley, however, turned into an excuse to be near Ernest. The Hemingways did not realize at first what was happening. Actually, Hadley was more worried at the moment about Lady Duff Twysden, a recent arrival from England, who seemed to be worshiped by every male in Paris. When Bill Smith arrived in Paris, however, he saw at once that Pauline was trying to steal Ernest from Hadley.

The quarrel with the Smith family had been patched up, and the Hemingways put Bill Smith up in their apartment and aggressively tried to find work for him. After Walsh refused to give Bill a job on *This Quarter,* Ernest broke off his friendship with Walsh.

A new friend, meanwhile, puzzled Ernest. *The Great Gatsby* was one of his favorite novels at the time, but he could not at first believe that the shy, well-dressed man with a midwestern accent who introduced himself as the author had really written it. It was even more puzzling when F. Scott Fitzgerald sought Ernest's friendship and guidance. Scott got drunk easily, and both he and his wife, Zelda, drank excessively, but Scott was puzzling drunk or sober.

Fitzgerald and several other friends encouraged Ernest to write a novel, but he repeatedly said that the novel was worn-out and overworked. In June 1925, however, just a few weeks before his twenty-sixth birthday, he wrote the first twenty-seven pages of "Along with Youth: A Novel." Based loosely on his war experiences, it included a romance with a Red Cross nurse, but he lost interest in it when the time approached for another vacation in Pamplona. This time, by including so many friends, Ernest turned the trip into a pilgrimage.

After leaving Bumby with a family in Brittany, Ernest and

Hadley, with Bill Smith and Don Stewart, arrived in northern Spain to fish for a week before the festival began. Meanwhile, Harold Loeb and Duff Twysden had begun a secret liaison before going to Pamplona. Ernest's plans had not included Duff or Pat Guthrie, another of her male companions. Duff, however, was always good company. Her carefree manner, natural charm, and love of male attention enlivened any party, and she could outdrink most of her companions.

Pamplona did not seem as exciting as Ernest remembered it, and he soon became envious of Duff's attentions to Loeb. Rivalry began the first morning in the amateurs' bullring. With brute strength, Ernest bulldogged an animal cowboy style, but the more agile Loeb stole the show by doing a handstand on the horns of a bull as it carried him from one side of the arena to the other.

In the afternoon, a perfect performance by Cayetano Ordoñez, the leading matador of the season, restored Ernest's spirits. He was also smugly pleased to see that several in his party, including Harold and Duff, were upset by the bloody goring of the horses. That night, Duff drank herself into a stupor, and Ernest showed his envy of Harold. This upset Don Stewart, who was further angered when Pat Guthrie borrowed money from him so he and Duff could pay their bills. Tensions crackled.

Emotions snapped one afternoon after Harold left Duff drinking alone in a café. She appeared at the hotel several hours later with a black eye, a cut forehead, and no memory of what had happened. Guthrie ordered Loeb to leave the party. Duff ordered him to stay. Ernest called Loeb a coward. Loeb challenged Ernest to a fistfight.

The cool air outside the hotel cooled their tempers and sobered them enough to make peace, but the incident had

In 1925, in the amateur bullring at Pamplona, Ernest, in white trousers and dark shirt, confronts a charging bull. (Hemingway Society)

destroyed their friendship. When the fiesta ended, the party scattered. Ernest and Hadley continued to Madrid to watch Ordoñez thrill the crowds again. He dedicated one of his bulls to Hadley and gave her one of its ears.

That evening, a thrilled Ernest began planning a novel with Ordoñez as the prototype for his hero. Soon, after he wove in the recent tension at Pamplona, however, the matador's role became a minor one. He disguised his friends thinly. Duff Twysden became Brett Ashley. Pat Guthrie became Mike Campbell, and Harold Loeb became Robert Cohn. Ernest created Jake Barnes, who like himself was an American newspaperman, and like himself was writing a novel. Brett and Jake's strange love affair soon became the focus of the book.

Although he and Hadley continued to go to the bullfights every afternoon, Ernest spent most mornings on the book.

When they followed Ordoñez to Valencia, they also found time to enjoy the beach. His enthusiasm for the novel, however, grew rapidly. With his firm longhand, he filled page after page of his notebooks. When he was not writing he thought about the story almost constantly.

On August 12 Hadley returned to France to get Bumby. She left Ernest writing feverishly in a Madrid hotel. Sometimes he wrote until three or four in the morning, slept a few hours, and then wrote again. After a week alone, he returned to Paris, where he continued at almost the same pace. On September 21, 1925, just a little more than two months after he began, Ernest completed the first draft. The manuscript filled six notebooks and part of a seventh.

Drained emotionally and physically, he went alone to Chartres to rest and try to think of a title. After discarding several ideas, he settled on a phrase from Ecclesiastes, a book of the Old Testament. "The sun also rises" refers to continuance of life despite the passing generations. This, Ernest decided, described his novel perfectly.

Back in Paris, he was eager to start revising, but there were several distractions. The first copies of *In Our Time* arrived along with generally good reviews. He was upset, however, that Liveright had printed just thirteen hundred copies. He thought it showed lack of faith. He was also angered by a reviewer who said one of the stories was as good or better than anything Sherwood Anderson might have written. It was meant as praise, but Ernest had developed a low opinion of his old friend's work.

No one can fully explain, however, why Ernest, with his own novel still to be revised, chose this time to write a satire of *Dark Laughter*, Sherwood Anderson's most recent book. Lampooning Anderson's style, Ernest wrote *The Torrents of*

Spring in no more than a few weeks. When he read the satire aloud to Dos Passos, Dos was amused but puzzled by Ernest's motivations. Hadley and Gertrude Stein were also puzzled. Hadn't Anderson helped Ernest get established in Paris? Wasn't he a friend? Pauline Pfeiffer was the only one who urged Ernest to submit the book for publication.

When Ernest sent the book to Liveright, some of his friends thought they understood what was happening. Perhaps Ernest wanted to change publishers. The contract he had signed for *In Our Time* gave Liveright the option to Ernest's next novel. As Anderson's publisher, Horace Liveright could never agree to publish a satire of his work. Rejection was almost certain, and rejection would free Ernest of any further obligation with Liveright.

Ernest never admitted such duplicity, but while on a skiing vacation in Schruns, he received word that Liveright had indeed rejected *Torrents*. Meanwhile, he was busy revising *The Sun Also Rises*.

Pauline joined them just before Christmas to take skiing lessons from Ernest. The snow was poor for skiing, however, and the three of them spent most of the holidays indoors. Although she remained Hadley's "friend," Pauline took advantage of the situation to win Ernest's affections. Meanwhile, after hearing from Liveright, Ernest decided to go to New York to find a new publisher.

He left Hadley and Bumby in Schruns while he and Pauline went to Paris. She was with him almost every hour until he sailed. Ernest arrived in New York on February 9, 1926, made a cordial break with Horace Liveright, and went at once to see Max Perkins at Charles Scribner's Sons. Thanks to Fitzgerald, Perkins had already seen some of Ernest's stories and written him a cordial letter. He now gave Ernest a warm

In 1926 Hadley and Ernest take Bumby walking on a mountain path in Schruns, Austria. (Hemingway Society)

welcome and offered a 15 percent royalty with a fifteen-hundred-dollar advance each on *Torrents* and the unfinished *The Sun Also Rises*. Ernest accepted the offers immediately.

With business taken care of, he began celebrating. He went to plays and looked up old friends. He met Dorothy Parker, Robert Benchley, and many other stimulating writers. He extended his stay from the planned seven days to nineteen days. Perhaps he wanted to put off the return to Europe and the domestic crisis waiting him there. He was in love with two women and did not know what to do about it.

Hadley and Bumby had still not returned to Paris, but Pauline was waiting there when Ernest arrived. He spent several days with his lover before guilt drove him to his family in Schruns. He still had more work to do on *The Sun Also Rises,* but emotional confusion made concentration difficult. Then Dos Passos arrived with Gerald and Sara Murphy, a popular, well-to-do couple who divided their time between Paris and the French Riviera. The visitors stayed in Schruns a week, putting Ernest in a very dark mood. He did get back to work, however, as soon as they left.

When he and Hadley returned to Paris at the end of March 1926, the revisions were finished. He hoped to relax, but a domestic storm was about to begin.

Chapter 9

Pauline

HADLEY BECAME AWARE HER MARRIAGE WAS IN trouble a few days after her return to Paris when Pauline and Virginia took her on a tour of the château country southwest of the city. Pauline was moody, and Hadley asked Virginia if it had something to do with Ernest. The sister said that Pauline and Ernest were very fond of each other.

Back in Paris, Hadley asked Ernest if he loved Pauline. The question was an emotional bomb. He yelled that she must not mention Pauline's name. Then he ran down the stairs in a rage. Hadley wept.

The scene did not dampen Ernest's creative energy. He wrote a short story about a couple in the Alps who were having marital problems. He also made plans to return to Spain, where he could work alone on more stories. Hadley and Bumby, who had a bad cold, would remain in Paris.

In Madrid in mid-May, Ernest found it so cold that he had to write in bed to stay warm. He completed the rough drafts of several stories, including "The Killers," about two Chicago gunmen looking for an ex-boxer who is marked for death.

Hadley, meanwhile, took the still ailing Bumby to the Murphys' at Cap d'Antibes. She hoped the Riviera weather would cure the boy's persistent cold. It was soon discovered, however, that Bumby had whooping cough. The Fitzgeralds, who were staying nearby, provided a small cottage where Hadley and Bumby could stay in quarantine. Ernest arrived early in June. By then, Archibald and Ada MacLeish had joined the Murphys and the Fitzgeralds, and party spirits were too high for Ernest to work.

His mood darkened after *Scribner's Magazine* rejected his story about the couple in the Alps, and *The Torrents of Spring* drew poor reviews. The critic for the *New York World* said Hemingway lacked the gift of parody. Meanwhile, Sherwood Anderson was irate.

On the Riviera, Ernest and Hadley might have patched up their marriage, but when Pauline arrived to help care for Bumby, she left the Hemingways no time to be alone together. In July, with Bumby healthy again, Pauline and the Murphys accompanied the Hemingways to Pamplona. Ernest was unhappy and confused. He still loved Hadley, but thanks to his infidelity and her pride, they agreed to separate.

On their return to Paris in August, Ernest moved into Gerald Murphy's studio, where he tried to concentrate on proof sheets for *The Sun Also Rises*. Hadley took rooms in Hôtel Beauvoir and agreed conditionally to a divorce. She said that if Ernest and Pauline were still in love after a hundred days of separation, she would give Ernest a divorce. Pauline sailed at once for New York to keep her side of the bargain. Ernest was still confused.

Once home in Piggott, Arkansas, it took Pauline four days to find the courage to tell her conservative, Catholic parents that she planned to marry a divorced man. Paul and Mary

Pfeiffer were shocked. When she heard the full story, the mother sided with Hadley. For a time, Pauline's only support came from her wealthy uncle Gus. Eventually, however, her parents gave in to the inevitable, and Pauline settled down to wait and write daily letters to Ernest.

Although still upset, Ernest found solace in work. *Scribner's Magazine* bought "The Killers" for two hundred dollars. Another story, "The Undefeated," had been selected for inclusion in *The Best Short Stories of 1926*. An English edition of *In Our Time* was being readied for publication, and negotiations had begun for an English edition of *The Sun Also Rises*, to be renamed *Fiesta*.

Archie and Ada MacLeish, his closest friends during this period, accompanied Ernest to prizefights and cycled and hiked with him. In late fall, Ernest and Archie went to Zaragosa, Spain, for the bullfights. Archie was the first of his friends to call Ernest "Pappy."

Although Archie's companionship helped, Ernest often fell into deep melancholy. Guilt over Hadley was acute. He thought of suicide. When Hadley found an apartment in Paris she asked Ernest to deliver her possessions there. He arrived with a loaded wheelbarrow, almost blind with tears. The experience, however, was not wasted. He wrote "A Canary for One" about an estranged couple seeking separate places to live. *Scribner's Magazine* promptly purchased it for $150.

Before the hundred days ended, Hadley left Bumby with Ernest and went to Chartres. From there she wrote Ernest saying he could begin divorce proceedings at once, and that he could visit Bumby whenever he wished. Ernest was so moved that he assigned all the royalties from *The Sun Also Rises* to Hadley.

The royalties promised to be substantial. Max Perkins

wrote that even though the book had been out just two months, it was already in its third printing. Reviews were generally good. The news, however, failed to cheer Ernest.

The novel was sending shock waves through Paris. Harold Loeb, who had been the model for the book's unattractive Robert Cohn, was rumored to be looking for Ernest with a gun. Actually Loeb was simply stunned and unable to guess what he had done to deserve such treatment from Ernest. Duff Twysden, who served as the model for Ernest's Brett Ashley, was also upset but would not show it. When she saw Ernest she joked that her only regret was that, contrary to his novel, she had not actually slept with the bullfighter.

Ernest's parents, who had already objected to both the subject matter and language of his short stories, were dismayed by the frank language and theme of the novel. Dr. Hemingway wrote that he liked healthier literature. Grace called the book the filthiest novel of the year. Ernest responded with an angry letter questioning the family's loyalty.

Meanwhile, the book made Ernest's reputation as a leading American author. The influential critic Edmund Wilson considered it the best novel written by anyone in Hemingway's generation. Young college men and women began modeling themselves after Brett and Jake. Demand for his short stories increased. The *Atlantic Monthly* paid $350, his best magazine price yet, for "Fifty Grand," another boxing story. Max Perkins asked for a collection of new stories that Scribner's could publish in the coming fall.

When Pauline returned to Paris in January 1927, her husband-to-be had become a celebrity. They went to Switzerland at once for a skiing vacation with Pauline's sister, Virginia, and the MacLeishes. The divorce became final on January 27. Pauline wanted to get married at once, but Ernest was not

72

so eager. He had not yet told his parents about the divorce or about Pauline. For a time, he was not actually sure he wanted to marry Pauline. He confided to a few friends that he would return to Hadley if she would have him. He went back to Paris twice during the winter to bring Bumby to the snow.

In mid-March he took a motoring trip to Italy. He needed time to think. At Rapallo he looked up the priest who had anointed him when he had been wounded in 1918. The meeting was more practical than sentimental. Ernest, who had to prove baptism as a Catholic to marry Pauline, decided that the priest's simple act was all the baptism he needed, but the written record that Pauline wanted did not exist. From Rapallo Ernest went to Pisa, Florence, and across the Apennines to Rimini.

Pauline wrote that she had found an apartment she liked and thought Uncle Gus Pfeiffer would be willing to pay the rent. Like a cheerful bride, she advised Ernest to get bachelor travels out of his system because once they were married he would always have her with him. Ernest was not so cheerful. During the trip, he stopped often to pray at religious shrines. Sometimes he cried. The Italian people, cheerless under Fascist rule, did not help Ernest out of his depression. He returned to Paris in time to bid Hadley and Bumby sad farewells. She planned to visit several friends in America before returning to France. Ernest did not know when he would see her again.

A new friendship with an American artist helped lift his spirits. Waldo Peirce, a jovial painter from Maine, had been an ambulance driver in France during the war. He spoke French and Spanish fluently. Ernest admired his energy and spirit, and when Peirce said *The Sun Also Rises* was a terrific novel, Ernest also gave his new friend credit for good taste in literature.

Ernest's spirits had fully revived by May 10, 1927, when he and Pauline were married in the Paris Church of Passy by a Catholic priest. They went to Grau du Roi, a small fishing village near the mouth of the Rhône, for a three-week honeymoon. Ernest fished, swam, and wrote. He had selected fourteen recent stories for Scribner's and decided to call the collection *Men without Women*. Unfortunately, near the end of the honeymoon, he cut his foot on the beach. The wound became infected, and when they returned to Paris he went to bed with a fever.

He recovered in ten days, in time for the annual trip to Spain. The Spanish vacation continued into the fall, and when he returned to Paris, stacks of mail waited his attention. Perkins reported that sales of *The Sun Also Rises* had passed twenty-three thousand. There were hundreds of fan letters praising the book. The mail, however, also included devastating reviews of *Men without Women*. British novelist Virginia Woolf, writing in the *New York Herald Tribune,* said Hemingway's talent had diminished as he became obsessed with his own virility. Other reviewers, while praising his talent and style, either lamented the vulgarity of his characters or his apparent lack of any governing philosophy. The comments were sincere and well-intended, but Ernest dismissed them all angrily. He was now unable to profit from criticism.

There were, however, other things beside reviews on his mind. Ernest had started another novel. Pauline was pregnant, and like Hadley, she wanted to have the baby in the United States. Ernest had just a few more months in France before he would have to go home again. He was not sure it was what he wanted.

This formal picture of Ernest was taken a few months before his return to the United States. (Hemingway Society)

Chapter 10

Key West

A SERIES OF MISHAPS, STARTING WITH THE INFECTED foot, plagued Ernest for several months. He and Pauline had planned to start a ski vacation well before the holidays. This suited Hadley perfectly. She had returned to Paris recovered from the divorce and looking radiant. She smiled at hints of a new romance and was delighted to put Bumby in Ernest's charge for several days.

Pauline, however, was miserable with morning sickness, and when Ernest came down with a serious cold, the Hemingways delayed their vacation. When he arrived in the Alps at last, Ernest first suffered a scratch on the pupil of his right eye, then a toothache, and finally a painful case of hemorrhoids. He took to bed for two days. When MacLeish arrived in mid-January, Ernest had recovered enough to ski, but the snow had a treacherous crust. After several painful falls, he gave up.

Back in Paris at the end of January, they found their water pipes frozen and their apartment without heat. Ernest went to bed with the flu. Worse was still to come. Early one March morning he got up to use the bathroom, and instead of pulling the cord that flushed the toilet, he pulled the cord that opened the skylight. The roof had rotted, and the entire skylight, casement, glass, and all, crashed onto Ernest's head. He fell unconscious, bleeding from a cut forehead. Although the gash was quickly stitched at a hospital, the accident left him depressed for days.

After writing forty-five thousand words, he abandoned the new novel. He also gave up on a short story. Eventually, however, enthusiasm grew for a new project. His war experiences in Italy and his love affair with Agnes von Kurowsky had been on his mind for several months. He had been thinking of Italy when he started "Along with Youth." After abandoning that project, he thought he might use the material for a short story. Each time he thought about it, however, the story grew. When the Hemingways boarded the ship for the journey home in mid-March, Ernest began to write. His head was still bandaged but his mind was clear and he worked with revived energy and enthusiasm.

His only major distraction was deciding where to live. The baby was not due until June. They needed a place to stay for two months. The much-traveled Dos Passos had recommended Key West, Florida, population ten thousand, as the ideal haven for a writer. The Hemingways decided to investigate. They were not disappointed. It was a sleepy Florida fishing village not yet overrun with tourists. Ernest loved the palms, flowering shrubs, and tropical mornings, and the cooling afternoon trade winds. Most of the old wooden homes had shaded porches that were both mysterious and inviting.

Ernest quickly fell into a routine. After a morning of writing, he could walk the long beaches, fish from the jetty, or simply watch the steady traffic of boats in and out of the harbor. The seamen and fishermen who drank and brawled in the cafés at night reminded Ernest of some of the characters

In April 1928 Ernest's parents came to Key West to meet his new wife. Here the two couples stand before the Ford roadster. (Hemingway Society)

in his own stories. Bra Saunders was a guide who knew every hot fishing spot on the coast. Charles Thompson, whose passion for hunting and fishing won Ernest's admiration at once, ran a shop that sold hardware, marine supplies, fishing tackle, and ice.

The elder Hemingways were vacationing in Florida, and Ernest invited them to Key West. He was shocked to see how his father had changed and was dismayed to learn that Ed Hemingway was suffering from diabetes and heart trouble. His hair was gray, his body frail, and he was tense and nervous. By contrast, Grace was in excellent health and eager to know her new daughter-in-law. The visit ended with everyone on good terms.

Ernest next invited Dos Passos, Waldo Peirce, and Bill Smith on a fishing trip. They hired Bra Saunders and his boat to take them to the Dry Tortugas. Peirce landed a six-foot tarpon after a forty-minute fight, and Ernest hooked a big sailfish. Although it got away, he was so excited that he came home determined to do more deep-sea fishing.

Meanwhile, he wrote faithfully. He and the pregnant Pauline rarely went out after dinner. There was little drinking and no late carousing to sap his creative energy. The productive period convinced him that Key West must one day be their home. Pauline agreed.

They left in May to visit Pauline's family in Piggott, Arkansas. The place seemed dull after Key West, and Pauline's parents were too conservative for Ernest's tastes. Her uncle Gus, however, was a delight. He had approved of Ernest since first meeting him in Paris. Gus Pfeiffer's controlling interest in a perfume company had given him wealth enough to indulge his large, generous spirit to the fullest. One of his wedding gifts for Pauline and Ernest was a yellow Ford runabout that Ernest loved.

Ernest wanted the baby to be born in Michigan, but his father wrote to say that medical facilities in St. Louis or Kansas City were far better. They picked Kansas City because of Ernest's friends there from his days on the *Star*. The Kansas heat of mid-June soon made them regret their decision. Luckily, they stayed with friends who had a swimming pool. Ernest tried to write, but as Pauline's time drew near, her discomfort grew.

Labor began on June 27. She was rushed to Research Hospital, where her pains continued through the night. Finally, after eighteen hours of labor, a nine-and-a-half-pound boy, Patrick, was delivered by cesarean section. Pauline's recovery was slow and painful. She could not eat and was unable to nurse. The heat continued. Ernest waited impatiently for ten days before Pauline was well enough to travel. Parents and baby returned to Piggott by train. As soon as Pauline and Patrick were settled with the Pfeiffers, however, Ernest returned to Kansas City, picked up his Ford, and drove into the Rocky Mountains.

After the demands of maternity and marriage, Ernest needed solitude. He also hoped to locate a guest ranch for the family, work on his book without distraction, and perhaps catch a few trout.

Early August found him poking around the Bighorn Mountains not far from Sheridan, Wyoming. He tried two guest ranches and did not like either of them, but when Pauline and Patrick arrived in Sheridan on August 18, Ernest was close to the end of the first draft of his Italian novel.

Both he and Pauline were ready to roam. They drove, fished, and investigated dude ranches for three weeks. They saw the Tetons and the Snake River. They did not find a guest ranch that suited them, but between them they had hooked six hundred trout. They returned to Piggott in good spirits.

After staying a month with the elder Pfeiffers, Ernest and Pauline left the baby with them and went to Chicago to visit friends. Next, after a brief stay with his parents in Oak Park, they went to Massachusetts to visit the MacLeishes. From there they went to New York, where Ernest conferred with Max Perkins.

Ernest had decided on *A Farewell to Arms* as the title for his new book. The phrase came from a verse by the English poet George Peale. Perkins liked the title and was eager to see the manuscript. Ernest, however, was not yet sure that it was good. He wanted several more weeks of rest before starting the revisions, and he would not begin until he returned to Key West. Through a friend, Ernest had already rented a house not far from Key West's east shore.

As he and Pauline drove south with the baby, he planned his writing campaign carefully. He had invited his sister Sunny to Key West to help Pauline with Patrick and to type the final draft as he completed revisions. The program, however, was delayed. No sooner had the Hemingways arrived in early December, than Ernest had to return to New York to meet Bumby, who was due by boat from France. Father and son had just started the return train trip to Florida on December 6 when a cable arrived from Oak Park. Ed Hemingway had died that morning. Ernest put Bumby in the care of a Pullman porter and left the train at Trenton, New Jersey. Then Ernest caught another train for Chicago. Not until he arrived in Oak Park did he learn that his father had committed suicide. Although Ed Hemingway had taken heavy financial losses on Florida real estate, the main cause of his depression was ill health. He shot himself in the head with a .32-caliber revolver.

After the funeral Ernest went home sadly with new responsibility. Grace was left with little money, and Ernest wrote several letters trying to enlist family help. He decided his own contribution would be one hundred dollars a month. Meanwhile, he began the revisions at last. He rose early and worked six hours each day. He did the rough typing. Sunny typed the final draft. When the job was finished, Ernest invited Max Perkins to come to Key West to collect the manuscript. Max arrived on February 1, 1929, to begin what he later described as the happiest week of his life.

Ernest took Max fishing every morning and did not bring

him home until midafternoon. Max read the manuscript avidly in his spare time. He had nothing but praise for *A Farewell to Arms,* and soon after returning to New York he persuaded the editors of *Scribner's Magazine* to pay a record sixteen thousand dollars for serial rights.

Ernest, however, still felt uncertain about the book. As before, he had relied heavily on real people and real events for his characters and his plot, perhaps too heavily. Agnes von Kurowsky was thinly disguised as nurse Catherine Barkley, who emerges as little more than a love object for the wounded hero. She is hardly worthy of Agnes, an intelligent and responsible nurse. The hero, of course, Lieutenant Henry, was modeled on Ernest himself.

Early in April the Hemingways sailed for France and were back in the old Paris apartment before the end of the month. Ernest wrote little, claiming that the demands of Pauline and Patrick, who were both sick, took all his energy. After both patients recovered, Patrick was put in a nursemaid's care, and Ernest and Pauline headed for Spain. He was still unable to write and the lack of production put him in a dark mood. Pamplona did not cheer him. In fact, he believed Spain had changed since his last visit. It seemed to him that prices on everything had gone up, and that American tourists could be seen everywhere, chewing gum and drinking Coca-Cola.

Ernest ate too much, drank heavily, and returned to Paris on September 20 with a kidney ailment. A doctor put him on a limited diet that did nothing to improve his mood.

Perkins sent glowing reviews of *A Farewell to Arms.* One reviewer compared the love story to *Romeo and Juliet,* and the book stood at the top of the best-seller list with twenty-eight thousand copies already sold.

Ernest's spirits, however, remained low. Paris, he said,

had also changed. Indeed, many of his former friends had taken Hadley's side in the divorce, and many others remembered what he had done to Harold Leob and Duff Twysden in *The Sun Also Rises*. When he regained his health, Ernest and Pauline began circulating among a new set of friends. Putting his social charm to work seemed to revive his spirits.

The Hemingways, who had introduced John Dos Passos to their old friend Katy Smith in Key West, were delighted when the two friends arrived in Paris in mid-December as man and wife. Ernest immediately organized a skiing vacation to celebrate. It was his last trip to the Alps for many years.

When they sailed for home on January 10, 1930, Ernest was in better spirits, but he decided he had seen his fill of Europe. Key West was going to look very good.

He and Pauline took over a large house on Pearl Street not far from the Key West Casino. Ernest, who had not done any serious writing for months, was interested in *Fortune* magazine's request for a bullfight article. Archie MacLeish was now working for *Fortune*. It might be fun, and the magazine was offering one thousand dollars.

First, however, he wanted to fish. He organized a trip to the Dry Tortugas for several friends. It turned into a great adventure.

Chapter 11

The Broken Arm

THE FISHING TRIP BEGAN WITH PROMISE. THE FIRST day, Max Perkins landed a fifty-eight-pound kingfish, one pound over the record, but a storm began to blow up before they reached the Dry Tortugas. When they arrived they had to take shelter in the abandoned harbor. The storm soon turned into a major blow. Ernest and his friends set up camp in a shed on an old pier. They lived there for seventeen days.

They ran out of ice, beer, canned food, coffee, liquor, and onions, nearly everything but fresh fish. When they finally returned to civilization, they all looked like bearded buccaneers. Perkins shaved and returned reluctantly to his New York office. Ernest tried to work on the bullfight article.

It soon became clear that he had a great deal to write on the subject, but he was not sure he wanted to put fiction aside to write a nonfiction account of bullfighting. The unusual spring heat made it hard to concentrate. He longed for the cool mountains of Wyoming.

When Katy and John Dos Passos came to Key West, Ernest gladly put the writing aside and organized another fishing trip. When that trip ended, a split right index finger gave him another excuse not to write. Once again, it was an unusual accident. He split the finger to the bone while working out on a punching bag. It took six stitches to close the wound, and it had not yet healed when Archie MacLeish arrived for a visit.

Meanwhile, Perkins was pleading for a new Hemingway story for the August issue of *Scribner's Magazine*. Ernest found time in May to write "Wine of Wyoming," based on a French family he and Pauline had met the previous summer. Perkins bought it for six hundred dollars and told Ernest to keep at it. But the story had increased his longing for Wyoming.

In June, after leaving Patrick with the Pfeiffers in Piggott and collecting Bumby in New York when he got off the boat from France, the Hemingways drove west.

This time, Ernest found a guest ranch he loved. Lawrence Norquist's L Bar T Ranch, about twelve miles from the old mining town of Cooke City, straddled the Clarks Fork Branch of the Yellowstone River, a river crawling with trout. Norquist put the new arrivals in a double cabin that was screened from the main lodge by a stand of lodgepole pines. The Hemingways moved in on July 13, 1930. From their windows they could see peaks that rose five thousand feet above the valley floor.

Ernest returned easily to a working routine, writing in the morning and fishing or horseback riding in the afternoon. He soon made friends with the wranglers. He preferred them to the company of the paying guests and usually ended the day in the bunkhouse, swapping yarns with Ivan Wallace and other cowhands. To his delight, they treated him as another member of their crew and called him "Pop."

When a neighboring rancher complained that a bear was killing his cattle, Wallace asked Ernest to help him take a bait horse into the high country. They shot the horse and left it in the sun, where Wallace said it would ripen quickly.

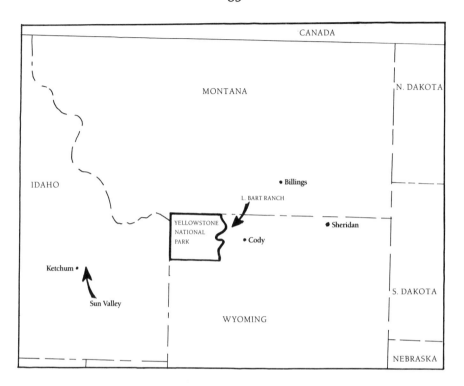

A few days later, when Ernest and three wranglers headed up the mountain to check the bait, he had another accident. His horse spooked and charged into a tangle of woods. Ernest fell out of his saddle. He got up bruised, scratched, and bleeding from a deep cut on his chin.

Wallace took Ernest by horse and car to Cody, Wyoming, home of the nearest doctor. They arrived at midnight, and the sleepy doctor had no anesthetic to ease the pain of the stitches. Ernest, however, like a true Hemingway hero, improvised by drinking he-man swigs from a bottle of whiskey until the wound was closed. He made sure, of course, to leave enough whiskey to wash down their breakfast.

Ernest recovered quickly and rode up the mountain again the evening after the accident. This time they found a brown bear feeding on the horse's carcass. Ernest killed the bear with a single shot. He and the wranglers skinned it and brought the pelt back to the ranch. A few days later, Ernest took Bumby up the mountain. They spotted another bear, and Ernest killed it, again with a single shot.

With his reputation as a hunter firmly established among guests and wranglers, Ernest returned from three days of fishing with ninety-two trout. His main regret, he told friends, was that he was neglecting his writing. In September, however, he returned to the bullfighting book with renewed enthusiasm.

On September 13, after Pauline and Bumby left for New York, Ernest and the wranglers packed into the high country for two weeks of hunting. He wanted mountain sheep, and the quest soon led him onto rocky slopes too steep for horses. While hiking above the tree line on his third day out, Ernest spotted four rams. He crept to within 350 yards before killing the oldest animal with one shot. Later, he killed a bull elk with one shot and declared the trip a success.

Back in his cabin, he worked until he had two hundred manuscript pages finished before he went bear hunting again with Ivan Wallace. He took another, longer break when Dos Passos arrived on October 21. It was late in the season, and Ernest was determined to make the hunt with Dos Passos a good one. Dos Passos soon discovered he was too nearsighted to hit anything, but he enjoyed the scenery and marveled at Ernest's enthusiasm. He was also impressed by the loyalty that the wranglers gave to Hemingway.

After ten days in the mountains, they returned to the ranch, loaded the Ford roadster, and on November 1 headed east with Ernest at the wheel, Dos Passos beside him, and wrangler Floyd Allington in the rumble seat. They had not gone far when another serious accident stopped them abruptly. One oncoming car trying to pass another forced Ernest to swerve off the narrow road. The Ford flipped and landed upside down in a ditch. Dos Passos and Allington were dazed but unhurt. Ernest, however, was pinned under the steering wheel, with a broken right arm. His friends pulled him free and caught a ride from a passing motorist to Billings, Montana, twenty-two miles to the east. Ernest, speechless with pain, rode the whole distance with his limp arm clamped between his knees.

Doctors at Billings's St. Vincent's Hospital said Ernest had suffered a spiral fracture just above his right elbow, a break that could not be set without surgery. Dos Passos wired the report to Pauline, who arrived in Billings in time for the operation.

It went well, but when Ernest woke, the pain was constant, and he raged at his fate when doctors told him he faced a month or more of immobility.

For several months, Ernest and Pauline had been considering a hunting trip to East Africa. Uncle Gus had offered to finance a safari for the Hemingways and at least three of their friends. Now the trip had to be postponed.

He couldn't write. He could not find a comfortable sleeping position. His arm seemed for a time to get worse. The elbow puffed up. The pain increased. The wound drained.

When Pauline returned to Piggott, Ernest's only faithful company was a portable radio, which he kept going far into the night. When the local station signed off, he searched for stations farther west. The last signal he could get came from Seattle, Washington. When that station signed off at 4:00 A.M., he had to wait for a morning program that came on the air from Minneapolis.

88

The Sisters of Charity of Leavenworth staffed the hospital, and Sister Florence soon became Ernest's favorite nurse. She believed that God shared her interest in baseball, and Ernest loved to hear her tell how God had answered her prayers during the recent World Series. He also got to know two patients across the hall. They were sugar-beet workers, a Russian and a Mexican, both of whom had been shot while drinking coffee in a café. The Mexican, whose gambling had won him an enemy, had been shot twice in the stomach. The Russian, an innocent bystander, had been hit in the thigh. The friends who came to visit them usually crossed the hall to sample Ernest's whiskey.

Ernest thought up a short story based on the nun, the gambler, and the radio, but several months would pass before he could write it.

He was finally discharged in time to join his family at Piggott for the Christmas holidays. His arm was still in a sling, and he was pale and unshaven, but he had hopes that 1931 would be a productive year. Soon after they returned to Key West, however, Ernest found that the accident had sapped more creative energy than he had imagined. Once again, idleness put him in low spirits.

He seemed to find fault in everything. When Sinclair Lewis, author of *Main Street* and *Babbitt*, praised Hemingway publicly, Ernest grumbled that he did not like Lewis and did not need his praise. He was even more upset when the critic Edmund Wilson, praising Hemingway's talent, wrote of the romanticism in *A Farewell to Arms*. Hemingway raged. Romantics were all fakes, he said, and he was no fake.

In a better mood, Ernest might have agreed with Wilson's appraisal. It was true that Ernest wrote in a realistic style, but his themes and his heroes were usually heavily romantic.

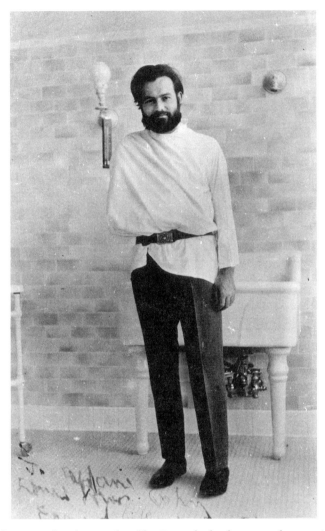

Tightly strapped and uncomfortable, Ernest had a long convalescence in Billings, Montana, after a 1930 auto accident. (Special Collections and Archives, Knox College Library, Galesburg, Illinois)

The literature of the era is crowded with flawed heroes like Jake Barnes and with characters in vain search of their destinies, like all members of the lost generation described in *The Sun Also Rises*. Frederic Henry and Catherine Barkley, fleeing the obligations of a wartime society they can no longer tolerate, are typically Romantic. And the ending of *A Farewell to Arms*, with Lieutenant Henry alone and desolate in a strange land, echoes the sentimentalism of Lord Byron and the other Romantic poets.

The Hemingways entertained many visitors in their rented Key West home. Pauline's sister, Virginia, and Ernest's sister Carol visited frequently. One of the wranglers, Chub Weaver, who had driven the repaired Ford down from Billings, was also a frequent quest. Grace Hemingway came for a few days. Lawrence and Olive Norquist visited in February. Max Perkins arrived in March.

So many joined the annual pilgrimage to the Dry Tortugas that Ernest rented a bigger boat. A storm again forced them into the harbor. They ran out of ice, and to Ernest's disgust, three hundred pounds of fish spoiled.

In April, with Ernest still not writing, Pauline announced that they could expect another baby in November. Ernest was pleased but said he needed to return to Spain before he could complete his bullfighting book. He and Pauline agreed that a summer trip was still possible. They could be home well before the baby arrived.

Meanwhile, the Hemingways had been eyeing an old house at 907 Whitehead Street. Before they left Key West, Uncle Gus arrived to inspect the house. It would take some work, Uncle Gus said, but if Ernest and Pauline liked, he'd be glad to buy it for them. The Hemingways said yes, and Uncle Gus, with his usual generosity, paid the full price of eight thousand and put the deed in Pauline's hands.

Chapter 12

Cuba

SPAIN WAS HEADED TOWARD CIVIL WAR. MOST OF Ernest's friends were Loyalists, sympathizing with the country's republican government. Almost all agreed, however, that the government had made serious mistakes and had failed to make promised reforms. Now the royalists, a conservative element that included landowners, the Catholic church, and much of the army, wanted to restore the monarchy.

In Pamplona, some 23,000 royalist demonstrators threatened to shut down the fiesta, but mass demonstrations were averted and the event opened peacefully. Spaniards, Ernest laughingly told his friends, would not let politics disrupt bullfights. Everywhere the Hemingways went during the summer of 1931, however, the talk focused on politics.

After the Pamplona festival ended, Ernest went to work on the long-delayed book. He compiled a glossary of bullfighting terms and pored over special bullfighting newspapers, collecting current reports to bring his book up-to-date. In mid-September the Hemingways picked up Patrick, who had been left with a nurse, and went to Paris for a brief stay. Ernest had just two more chapters to write when they sailed for home.

Sailing with them were Don Stewart and his wife, Bertha. She was also pregnant and gave Pauline company while Don and Ernest talked into the late hours each evening in the ship's bar. They also enjoyed the company of Jane Mason, the pretty wife of an airline executive. In New York, Ernest gave Perkins a progress report on the book soon to be called *Death in the Afternoon*. Then the Hemingways headed for Kansas City to wait for the second baby.

Pauline gave birth to a nine-pound boy on November 12, 1931. Gregory Hancock Hemingway, soon shortened to "Gigi" or "Gig," was delivered by another cesarean section, and doctors warned Pauline not to have any more children. Ernest lost hope of one day having a daughter.

After a week in Piggott in early December, the Hemingways went to Key West to take possession of the house Uncle Gus had purchased for them. Carpenters and plumbers were still at work, and the rooms were filled with packing cases. The chaos was too much for a weary Pauline. She went to bed exhausted. Ernest developed a sore throat. Patrick swallowed ant poison and had to go through a twenty-six-hour ordeal of forced vomiting. Christmas passed almost unnoticed.

Peace was soon restored, however, and Ernest finished the bullfighting book the second week in January. Then he began planning the African trip for the coming fall. He selected an arsenal of two rifles, one 12-gauge shotgun, and a Colt Woodsman .22-caliber pistol. He hired Philip Percival, one of the most experienced white hunters in Kenya, and he warned his friends to get ready.

The trip would be very expensive, costing perhaps as much as $22,000, but Uncle Gus was willing to pay it all.

While travel plans took shape, Ernest worked on another

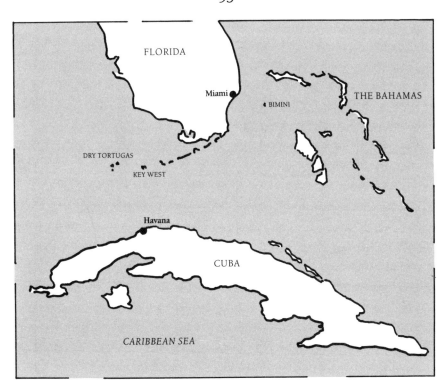

collection of short stories that Perkins wanted to publish in the fall. Eventually to be called *Winner Take Nothing,* it would have fourteen stories, including "After the Storm," based on Bra Saunders's discovery of a sunken ship.

In February and again in March, Ernest went fishing at the Dry Tortugas. In April, he and Joe Russell, owner of Sloppy Joe's Bar in Key West, went to Havana, Cuba, in Russell's thirty-two-foot boat. Cuba was a great discovery for Ernest. What was to be a two-week visit turned into a two-month stay. There were several attractions. He could live in Havana's Ambos Mundos Hotel for two dollars a day. Marlin fishing, which Ernest described as one of the world's most challenging sports, was superb. And Jane Mason, whom he had met on his recent Atlantic crossing, was living in Havana with her husband, a representative of Pan American Airways. Jane was delightful company for a day of fishing.

Ernest caught nineteen marlin during his stay. He also corrected proof sheets for *Death in the Afternoon* and wrote "A Way You'll Never Be," a short story based on his war experiences in Italy.

By the time he returned to his family in Key West in June, he had decided to postpone Africa for another year. He said his eyes had been bothering him, but the prospect of another season in Wyoming and the promise of more fun in Cuba probably had greater influence on his decision.

Ernest spent the latter part of June in bed with bronchial pneumonia. His fever peaked at 102 degrees and he was still not fully recovered when the time came to drive west.

On the way to the Norquist ranch, Pauline was saddened by the sight of the many Americans put out of work by the Great Depression. Ernest showed little sympathy. He said he had been poor in France all through the twenties while Americans at home reaped the profits of the boom years.

They reached the ranch on July 12, 1932, and Ernest soon fell into a working routine. On a normal day, after a big breakfast, he would watch Ivan Wallace saddle horses for the morning ride. Then, as the guests rode out, Ernest would go to the cabin and write. Most afternoons he and Pauline went riding or fishing.

When Gerald and Sara Murphy, friends from the Paris years, arrived with their two children early in September, Ernest took Gerald to the high country and killed a mule for bear bait. A few days later Charles Thompson, a friend from Key West, arrived for a month of hunting with Ernest. Each killed an elk, and Charles shot a bear. Ernest felt compelled to kill a bear of his own to even the score, but he did not see one until October 11. Although his first shot only wounded the animal, it left such a clear trail of blood that Ernest tracked it down easily for the finishing shot.

Perkins wrote that reviews of *Death in the Afternoon* were generally good, but when they began to reach Ernest he could not agree. One reviewer thought Ernest's enthusiasm for bullfighting was childish and morbid. Another accused Ernest of he-man posturing. Still another called Ernest that hateful thing—a romantic.

A few weeks later, when Paramount Pictures released its production of *A Farewell to Arms,* Ernest was furious to discover that the scriptwriters had given the story a happy ending. Although Gary Cooper and Helen Hayes did fine jobs in the starring roles, Ernest declared it a bad film.

Back in Key West at the end of October, Ernest greeted Bumby, who had come to spend the winter with the family. The poet Evan Shipman, whom Ernest and Hadley had known in their first days in Paris, would arrive in January to serve as Bumby's private tutor.

Ernest was eager to get back to work, but early in 1933, he took a solo trip to New York to talk business with Perkins and with Maurice Speiser, now serving as his agent. He renewed his friendship with American bullfighter Sidney Franklin, whom Pauline and Ernest had cheered in Spain during the summer of 1931. Ernest also met Arnold Gingrich for the first time. A book collector and Hemingway fan, Gingrich was about to launch an influential monthly magazine called *Esquire.* He soon offered Ernest $250 a month for a regular feature on hunting, fishing, or anything else he wanted to write. Ernest accepted the offer.

Meanwhile, back in Key West, Ernest began a story about a tough Key West fisherman he called Harry Morgan. To support himself and his family during the hard times of depression, Morgan picked up extra money smuggling illegal whiskey in from Cuba in his fishing boat. Although he liked his character, Ernest would have a long struggle with the story.

Shipman, when not tutoring Bumby, struggled to bring order to Ernest's office. It was almost impossible. Files overflowed with unanswered fan mail, but Ernest would throw nothing away. Even old laundry lists had to be saved. Shipman could not understand how Ernest could work in so much clutter.

The Harry Morgan story grew longer and longer. Ernest told Perkins at the end of February that it was almost finished, but it continued to grow.

Distractions frustrated him. He took another solo trip to New York to discuss a film version of *Death in the Afternoon*. Although he approved of the project, he did not think the film would ever be made. Soon after returning to Key West he was upset by the news that his sister Carol had married John Gardner in Vienna, Austria. Ernest, who did not like Gardner and had forbidden the marriage, said he would never mention his sister's name again.

Next, he was further upset by Gertrude Stein's memoirs, disguised under the title *The Autobiography of Alice B. Toklas*. Gertrude, who had remained angry at Ernest for lampooning Sherwood Anderson, wrote that she and Anderson had created Hemingway and were now both a little proud and a little ashamed of their work. What made Ernest seethe, however, was a passage in which Gertrude called him "yellow."

In April, Ernest chartered Joe Russell's boat and crossed to Cuba to fish for marlin. He hired veteran fisherman Carlos Gutiérrez as guide and began catching an average of one marlin a day. He established a schedule. He rose with the sun, showered, donned khaki shirt and trousers and a pair of moccasins, and then strode out to buy the papers, which he read over a light but leisurely breakfast. Meanwhile, Joe Russell and Carlos Gutiérrez fueled the boat and were ready to cast off the lines as soon as Ernest came aboard.

If marlins were running, Ernest began trolling soon after the boat left the harbor. If there was no promise of fish, however, he was content to anchor off a beach to swim and doze in the sun. Ernest's main regret of the season was that none of his friends could join him. Jane Mason was recuperating from an auto accident. Dos Passos was in a Baltimore hospital with rheumatic fever. Ernest sent him one thousand dollars to encourage his recovery, and continued to fish alone.

The June issue of the *New Republic* came out with an article by Max Eastman called "Bull in the Afternoon," a good-natured spoof of *Death in the Afternoon*. The humor was wasted on Hemingway, particularly when Eastman asked why Ernest had to engage in "juvenile romanticism" whenever he wrote about Spain. The critic also wondered if Ernest wore false hair on his chest.

Fishing was a solace. Early in July, he battled a huge marlin for an hour and a half. Gutiérrez had to douse Ernest with water to keep him from overheating, and several times Ernest would have been pulled over the stern if Gutiérrez had not clasped his arms around Ernest's waist and held him. The fish finally snapped the rod and broke free, but Ernest was proud of his part in the struggle.

It may have been soon after this experience that Gutiérrez told Ernest the sad story of a native fisherman who fought a huge marlin for hours only to lose it to sharks. Ernest was fascinated with the tale and could not get it out of his mind. One day, he was sure, it would make a fine story.

Chapter 13

Africa

THE FIRST LEG OF THE LONG-PLANNED AFRICAN TRIP began on August 7, 1933, when Ernest, Pauline, Bumby, and Pauline's sister, Virginia, sailed from Havana, Cuba, aboard *Reina de la Pacifica*. Charles Thompson, a Key West pal who was to be part of the safari, would join them in Paris. Ernest's party had a noisy Cuban send-off.

Fighting to overthrow the Cuban dictator, Gerardo Machado, was in full swing, and the Hemingways departed to the rattle of gunfire. After a few hours at sea, news came over the ship's radio that Machado had fled the country.

While at sea, Ernest wrote a new opening for his Harry Morgan story by inventing a revolutionary gun battle on the streets of Havana. Virginia read it and said it seemed so real that she believed that it had actually happened. Ernest was pleased.

The ship landed at Santander, Spain. Pauline and Virginia took Bumby to Hadley in Paris while Ernest remained in Spain to follow the bulls. The political situation upset him. Poverty among the peasants was worse than ever, but the promised reforms had not come. Civil war, Ernest concluded, was inevitable.

Nevertheless, he enjoyed his stay. He wrote almost every morning. He went wild boar hunting. He also swam across Madrid's cold Manzanares River as Spaniards watched in amazement. The bullfights were a disappointment. The matador Sidney Franklin, whom he hoped to see, had not yet recovered from his most recent goring.

When Ernest arrived in Paris, however, he was in high spirits. He delighted in showing Charles Thompson the city, and he felt good about Hadley. She had just remarried, and Ernest liked her husband. Paul Scott Mowrer, European correspondent for the *Chicago Daily News,* was about to go home to become editor of the paper. The marriage would be good for both Hadley and Bumby.

He was dismayed to learn that Ezra Pound, now a full-time resident of Italy, was lecturing in Milan on the benefits of Mussolini's fascism. In Paris, the French spoke fearfully of another great war. Ernest agreed that Hitler and Mussolini would certainly cause trouble. This time, however, Ernest said the United States must not get involved in the conflict.

Early reviews of *Winner Take Nothing* upset him. One critic wrote that Hemingway should stop writing about sports and give his attention to more important things. Another said his stories interested adolescents more than adults. The reviews, however, did not diminish his creativity. Before leaving Paris, he finished the Harry Morgan story and sent it to *Cosmopolitan.*

Thompson, Pauline, and Ernest sailed from Marseilles in southern France on November 22. The weather at first was cold and wet, but as they passed through the Suez Canal and entered the Red Sea, the heat became oppressive. Ernest and Charles spent much of the time playing checkers in the blaze of the sun, disdaining the awnings that had been rigged to shade the passengers.

In Mombasa, the main port of Kenya, the heat and humidity were almost unbearable. The only relief came after their train began to climb toward Nairobi, which was located at a much higher elevation and was cooler than the coast. Twenty miles south of Nairobi by car they arrived at the Percival ranch, where they unpacked their gear and waited for Philip Percival to return from an earlier safari.

They hunted gazelles, impalas, and guinea fowl on the nearby Kapiti Plains, but the outings left the hunters exhausted. They were grateful to have time to adjust to the altitude. When Percival arrived, he and Ernest took to each other at once. Ernest asked intelligent questions, remembered what he was told, and showed unbounded enthusiasm. Noting Ernest's glasses, however, Percival feared that his new friend might not be a very good shot. Ernest soon put that fear to rest.

On December 20, 1933, the party began the two-hundred-mile drive to Arusha in Tanganyika Territory (now Tanzania). Mount Kilimanjaro, over nineteen thousand feet high, dominated the eastern horizon. The Serengeti game preserve, their immediate destination, lay to the south. They had two lorries, doorless vehicles that seated six with room left over for their camping gear. Ben Fourie had joined the party as an assistant hunter and a mechanic. Native gun bearers and drivers completed the crew.

M'Cola, Ernest's gun bearer, was one of the few men indifferent to Ernest's charm. It seemed that nothing could change the passive expression of his wrinkled face.

Ernest loved the country, saying again and again that it was far better than anything he had read about it. The variety of the game and the size of the herds made it a hunter's heaven. In the first ten days they shot waterbuck, bushbuck, eland, antelope, two kinds of gazelle, and two leopards. The country was also famous for amoebic dysentery. It soon singled out Ernest and spoiled his fun. For the first few days, he tried to keep hunting, but he was too uncomfortable to enjoy it. By mid-January it became clear he needed medical care. Percival radioed for a plane to fly Ernest back to Nairobi for treatment.

Fatty Pearson, not at all fat and one of the best bush pilots in Africa, landed his two-seater plane on a hastily cleared field and flew Ernest back to civilization. It was not a pleasant experience, but ill as he was, he remembered it clearly and would one day use it skillfully in "The Snows of Kilimanjaro," one of his best African stories.

In Nairobi he was put to bed in a comfortable room at the New Stanley Hotel, where injections quickly restored his health. He stayed in bed while he wrote a safari article for *Esquire* and caught up on his mail. Perkins reported that despite poor reviews twelve thousand copies of *Winner Take Nothing* had been sold. *Cosmopolitan* offered $5,500 for the Harry Morgan tale, Ernest's top price to date for a single story.

On January 23, he rejoined the hunters in the hills south of Ngorongoro Crater, where the chief prey were sable antelope, kudu, and rhinoceroses. A local tracker whom Ernest called "Droopy" joined M'Cola on the hunt.

Hilly terrain forced them to hunt on foot. Ernest thought this a great improvement over the lorries. Meanwhile, Ernest and Percival, in their evening discussions around the campfire, discovered that they both put great importance on courage. After Ernest's steel nerves and a deadly eye won Percival's respect, the hunter told candid stories about clients who had either lost their nerve or found it during a hunt. Ernest filed the stories away in his memory for future use.

Competition with Thompson caused tension in the camp. One day, after killing a rhinoceros with a remarkable, three-

Ernest killed his first lion on the Serengeti Plain in January 1934. (Hemingway Society)

hundred-yard shot, Ernest returned to camp to find that Thompson had just killed a much bigger rhino. Ernest fell into another dark mood. Thompson had already shot the biggest lion, the biggest waterbuck, and the biggest buffalo.

The friendship with Thompson grew particularly strained when he shot a fine kudu buck long before Ernest even saw one of the elusive animals. He could not hide his disappointment, and his spirits were not restored until near the end of the trip, when he came back to camp with two fine kudu, both much bigger than Thompson's.

The rainy season brought an end to their hunting two weeks before their boat was to sail. To avoid an idle wait, Ernest organized a deep-sea fishing excursion on the Indian Ocean. They chartered a boat and made headquarters in a hotel at Malindi, just up the coast from Mombasa. The boat's engines were in such poor repair that the top speed was four miles an hour, but they managed to hook amberjacks, kingfish, dolphins, sailfish, and several other species. It was a satisfactory venture. Ernest had fished a new ocean, and he had introduced Percival to a new sport.

They sailed from Mombasa and docked at Villefranche, France, on March 18. The Hemingways spent a week in Paris renewing friendships. They saw James Joyce and Sylvia Beach.

In her bookstore, Miss Beach introduced Ernest to Katherine Anne Porter, whose popularity in America threatened to rival Hemingway's. The two stared at each other silently for several seconds. Then, without a word, Ernest abruptly walked out of the store.

During a later visit to the bookstore, Ernest had his first look at "The Dumb Ox," a critic's attack on Hemingway's anti-intellectualism. It put Ernest in such a rage that he shattered a vase with his fist. He soon turned contrite, however, and insisted on giving Beach 1,500 francs to replace it.

Homeward bound on *Ile de France,* Ernest met and impressed Marlene Dietrich. The glamorous actress was too superstitious to sit at a table where she would have made the thirteenth guest. Ernest rose from another table to join the party and make the fourteenth. His friendship with Dietrich continued until the end of his life.

On a brief stopover in New York, Ernest and Pauline took a cab to a Brooklyn shipyard. The time had come, he decided, to have his own fishing boat. He ordered a thirty-eight-foot cabin cruiser to be delivered in thirty days to Miami, Florida. Total cost was $7,500. Ernest covered the $3,300 down payment with money advanced from Gingrich on future *Esquire* articles.

Ernest could hardly wait to get home. He not only had

much to write, but he also wanted to prepare for the arrival of the cruiser. He had decided to christen it *Pilar*.

April in Key West was alive with visitors. John and Katy Dos Passos, Gerald and Sara Murphy, and several other friends were eager to fish. Ernest rented Bra Saunders's boat on an every-other-day schedule and took his friends into the Gulf Stream. His creative mind was not idle. The book on Africa, he decided, would be a nonfiction story told with all the narrative devices of the novel. It was a difficult challenge, but when he finally began writing, he mastered it skillfully.

Before his own boat arrived, Ernest took Dos Passos to Havana for a brief visit. It was too early in the season for marlin, but Ernest wanted to see how his friends had survived the revolution. As he feared, despite Machado's downfall, the political situation in Cuba remained unstable.

Early in May, Ernest and Bra Saunders went to Miami to accept delivery of *Pilar* and bring her to her home port. She was all Ernest dreamed, a beautiful boat, black with varnished woodwork, and a top speed of sixteen knots. The cabin was big enough to sleep six.

For several weeks, Ernest took *Pilar* on trial runs almost every afternoon. In the mornings, he curbed his new-boat enthusiasm to make a good start on the African book. He decided that it must not just describe a great adventure. It had to convey his zest for life.

Chapter 14

Bimini

IN MID-JULY 1934, WHEN CARLOS GUTIÉRREZ WROTE from Cuba to say marlins were running, Ernest declared a fishing holiday. After three months of steady work he had completed two hundred pages of the African book and he felt satisfied. What pleased him most was his ability to relate various parts of the African landscape to his moods.

The writing had brought his own behavior under the stress of hunting into focus, and he believed he had acted with calm, grace, and confidence, just as a Hemingway hero should act. It made him proud.

It was difficult to find a crew for *Pilar*. Ernest reluctantly enlisted Arnold Samuelson, a hopeful author who had come from Minnesota to interview him. Samuelson knew nothing about boats, but *Pilar* made the crossing to Cuba without difficulty.

As soon as he docked, Ernest once again hired Gutiérrez as fishing guide. Later, he invited two scientists aboard. Charles Cadwalader, director of the Academy of Natural Sciences of Philadelphia, and Henry W. Fowler, the academy's chief ichthyologist, were spending the season studying marlins. Ernest, with his keen observation and precise memory, related valuable information about their feeding and migratory habits. And he also caught many specimens for the scientists to measure and dissect. Other guests included Jane Mason and her husband, Grant.

Early in September, although the marlin season was at its height, Ernest returned to Key West to give full attention to the African book. He brought it close to completion in just a few days. Then he hurried back to Havana. Although others were catching fish, Ernest had little luck. One day he chased a pod of whales and tried to harpoon one of them. The harpoon stuck just behind the animal's blowhole. Ernest got ready to shoot it in case it tried to dive, but the whale stayed near the surface until the harpoon fell free.

In late October, Ernest piloted *Pilar* back to Key West in time to greet John and Katy Dos Passos and then take to bed with a cold. Dos Passos, who once remarked that he had never known an athletic man who spent more time in bed than Ernest, was amused when the household gathered in the host's bedroom for evening cocktails.

On November 16, with 492 manuscript pages completed, Ernest declared the African book finished. He called it *Green Hills of Africa* and wrote Perkins that it was his best work yet. He immediately wrote another article for *Esquire* and started a new short story. Then he drove his family to Arkansas to spend the holidays with Pauline's family. It rained during most of the ten days he spent there, and he returned to Key West moody and ill at ease. He was soon in bed again, this time with a recurrence of African dysentery.

He had regained his health by mid-January when Max and Louise Perkins arrived. Although the editor praised *Green Hills of Africa,* he could offer no more than five thousand dollars for serial rights from *Scribner's Magazine*. Ernest, who had expected ten thousand dollars, accepted the offer with reluctance.

With the depression easing, tourists had begun coming to Key West again. Many were eager to see the famous author, and Ernest let himself be seen. He walked out almost daily, either to Sloppy Joe's or to the docks. When he went to sea, he stood proudly at the helm of his cruiser. With his green eyeshade, tattered shirt, and bloodstained trousers, Ernest was clearly a member of the Gulf Stream brotherhood. No one mistook him for a tourist.

On April 7, with John and Katy Dos Passos, Ernest began his first trip to Bimini in the Bahamas. Another freak accident turned them back. It happened after Ernest tried to shoot a shark he had hooked and gaffed. He nearly emptied his pistol into the fish, but the gaff broke, the shark escaped, and Ernest was left gaping at his legs. They streamed blood. Somehow he had managed to put bullets through both his calves. Back at Key West a doctor treated the wounds and sent Ernest to bed for a week.

His legs were still bandaged and sore when he took *Pilar* across 230 miles of open water to reach Bimini without further incident. Although several expensive yachts lay in port, and Pan America Airways had a seaplane dock there, the island in 1935 was still quiet. When Pauline arrived by plane, she decided Bimini would be ideal for the children, and flew back to get them. While Ernest fished for tuna, John and Katy Dos Passos, Pauline, and the children swam and collected seashells.

After Ernest lost a hugh fish to a school of ravenous sharks, he returned to harbor bent on revenge. One of the yachtsmen owned a Thompson submachine gun, and Ernest bought it. Next time he went to sea, he was trigger-happy. One of the others hooked a huge marlin, but before he could get it into

Ernest discovered Bimini in 1935 and soon began landing prize catches, in-cluding this giant swordfish. (Hemingway Society)

the boat, Ernest began spraying the sea with bullets. Instead of chasing sharks away, the splashes attracted them, and they soon destroyed the prize fish. Ernest refused to admit that he had done anything wrong.

Late in May, Ernest started boasting that he could beat all challengers at boxing. His first victim was New York publisher Joseph Knapp. As usual, Ernest landed the first power punches. He stunned Knapp with two left hooks and dropped him with a roundhouse right. Knapp was still unconscious when his crewmen carried him back to his yacht. The fight had lasted just a few seconds.

After the Knapp fight, Ernest put out a challenge to the natives, offering $250 to anyone who could last three rounds with him. His first challenger was Willard Saunders, said to be the strongest man on Bimini. Saunders wanted to fight barefisted. Ernest agreed and knocked him out in a minute and a half. A second challenger failed to survive the second round, but the natives kept trying. There was usually at least one boxing match a week while Ernest was at Bimini.

While at the island, Ernest read proof sheets for *Green Hills of Africa* and wrote an article for *Esquire,* but he did little other work. In mid-August he took the *Pilar* back to Key West for an overhaul and learned that the engines needed so much work that he would have to postpone his fall trip to Cuba. It was just as well. The Hemingways were barely resettled at Whitehead Street when the first hurricane of the season gathered strength east of Key West. *Pilar* was not yet hauled out, and Ernest moored it with heavy line in the most sheltered corner of the harbor he could find. Then he went home and nailed up the storm shutters.

On September 2 the barometer dropped and the winds began. Ernest slept until midnight, when shrieking wind and lashing rain woke him. He left the house and struggled to the harbor through downed trees and power lines. He found *Pilar* was safe and stayed on her until dawn. Then he went home, stripped off his wet clothes, gulped down a glass of whiskey, and fell into a deep sleep.

He woke to tragic news. The Civilian Conservation Corps, created to provide federal jobs during the depression, had work camps on Upper and Lower Matecumbe keys. The camps received the full force of the storm, and almost a thousand men, many of them World War I veterans, had been drowned. As soon as the sea calmed, Ernest hired Bra Saunders and his boat to cruise up to the devastated area and see what could be done. At Lower Matecumbe, the storm had smashed an eighty-five-foot steel radio tower. Bodies, many bloated, lay everywhere. Ernest had not seen so much death since the Piave Valley in 1918. Two women who had owned the local sandwich shop had been stripped naked by the storm and tossed into the trees. Ernest was horrified and blamed the government for the disaster. Back in Key West he promptly wrote an article for the *New Masses,* describing the devastation and saying a timely evacuation could have avoided the tragedy.

Many readers saw the article as the awakening of Hemingway's political involvement, but Ernest maintained that writers should not be political. He claimed that writing was too demanding to allow political diversion.

Green Hills of Africa, to Ernest's dismay, brought mixed reviews. Although several liked the descriptions and excitement of the adventure, influential critics such as Edmund Wilson found little to praise. Ernest raged.

He said the critics had ganged up against him. He complained that Scribner's had overpriced the book and failed to promote it properly. When he calmed down, he went to work on another Harry Morgan story.

Chapter 15

Off to War

HE ENDED THE SECOND HARRY MORGAN STORY WITH his wounded hero dumping a cache of illegal rum at the mouth of a river. He began the third one immediately, but did not get far before he went into a slump accompanied by the usual ill temper.

Early in 1935 he broke a toe when trying to kick open his garden gate. He was still limping when Waldo and Alzira Peirce arrived with hyperactive twin sons. Ernest, whose own children were mostly under the care of Pauline or a nursemaid, thought Waldo's boys needed more discipline. Waldo laughed at the suggestion.

Harry Payne Burton of *Cosmopolitan,* who came to Key West in March, turned down a bullfighting story but offered Ernest $40,000 for the serial rights to his next novel and $3,000 to $7,500 for stories. Feeling encouraged, Ernest wrote diligently through the rest of the spring, producing some of his finest stories, including "The Short Happy Life of Francis Macomber." For this plot and these characters, he drew heavily on the hunting yarns Philip Percival had told him in Africa. Ernest said that his hero, a coward who finds courage, and Margot, his shrewish wife, were both "invented from real people." Descriptions of lion and buffalo hunting were based on his own experience.

When the story was finished, Ernest decided he had earned a Cuban vacation. He made the crossing on the *Pilar* with Jane Mason and Joe Russell. Pauline arrived in Havana by air.

It was not a successful vacation. *Pilar* had engine trouble. Fishing was poor. Ernest took out his frustration on Carlos Gutiérrez, whose hearing and eyesight were both failing. Ernest criticized Carlos for his limitations so harshly that his old friend frequently cried.

To everyone's surprise, Carlos later accepted Ernest's invitation to join the crew during the trip to Bimini. They made that crossing in a June storm. Ernest stayed at the helm all night, guiding his boat through heavy seas and bringing her safely into Bimini harbor. Although he bragged about the achievement, he confessed that he had been frightened.

Ernest's boxing and fishing feats had made him famous throughout the Bahamas, and most of the yachtsmen were eager to associate with him. Ernest, however, was cautious about making too many friends among the wealthy. In a current Harry Morgan story, he was contrasting the rich with the poor. He feared that the yachtsmen of Bimini might damage his image as the tough kid who had suffered poverty.

He was still at work on the third Harry Morgan story when Gingrich flew to Bimini for a conference. The editor suggested that the three stories be brought together into one novel. Ernest liked the idea at once and praised Gingrich for his literary judgment. The project, however, was to cause Ernest his greatest frustration so far as a writer.

Meanwhile, he struck up a friendship with Marjorie Rawlings, author of *The Yearling,* who was vacationing with friends in Bimini. Like others, she was puzzled by Ernest's conflicting nature. He had immense talent, yet he was very defensive about his work. He was big and gentle, yet capable of knocking people down. He liked blood sports but was one of the most sensitive writers she had ever met.

Ernest explained that hunting and fishing, which he had been doing all his life, offered an escape from the most difficult of trades. Although nothing could be more satisfying than writing when it went well, the difficulties would have driven him crazy if he had not had the release of outdoor sports.

When Ernest returned to Key West in mid-July, proofs for another African story he had written that spring were waiting for him. "The Snows of Kilimanjaro" tells of a writer who is dying of gangrene in a remote hunting camp. As his rich wife nurses him during the long wait for a rescue plane, the writer reviews his past. The story gave Ernest the chance to draw much from his own past, including many adventures and friends. He ungenerously described F. Scott Fitzgerald as a writer ruined by his fascination with wealth.

When the story was printed in *Esquire,* a deeply hurt Fitzgerald wrote Ernest a brief note asking him to lay off. Ernest said he was surprised by the reaction because Scott himself had said publicly that he was finished as a writer. As far as Fitzgerald was concerned, however, Ernest was finished as a friend.

In the last week of July 1936, the long-expected civil war broke out in Spain, but Ernest did not let the news change his plans for another trip to Wyoming. Spain, however, was much on his mind when he and Pauline drove into the L Bar T Ranch on August 10. When he found that there was only one of his old wrangler friends still on the staff, Ernest began feeling restless. The place did not seem the same.

A letter from Dos Passos reported that the artist Luis Quintanilla had become an officer in the Loyalist army and taken part in an attack on the rebel garrison during the first hours of the war. The story helped convince Ernest that he must go to Spain.

Meanwhile, Norquist had killed some mules in the high country for bear bait, and Ernest had hopes for a grizzly. His chance came sooner than expected. One afternoon, when he was headed up the trail to check the bait, three grizzlies crashed out of the woods just in front of him. His first shot knocked the largest bear down. As the two other bears ran for cover, he felled one of them with another shot. Then, the first bear scrambled up and ran. Ernest chased it into a stream and killed it with a shot in the neck as it tried to climb the far bank.

A proud Ernest insisted that night on cooking bear steak sandwiches for his friends. Although the meat was too tough and undercooked to bring any raves, Ernest ate all of his sandwich with gusto.

He worked on the Harry Morgan novel with little success. Combining the three stories was more difficult than antici-pated. When he and Pauline headed back to Key West, how-ever, he thought he could finish the book in a few more weeks. Then he would go to Spain. But he was still struggling with the book when he was approached by the North American Newspaper Alliance to cover the revolution. Ernest accepted, saying he would go as soon as he finished the book.

Both Perkins and Pauline opposed his decision. She was only slightly relieved when matador Sidney Franklin agreed to make the trip with Ernest and try to keep him out of danger.

Meanwhile, Ernest fell in love. He was in Sloppy Joe's one afternoon when the blond and beautiful Martha "Marty" Gellhorn came in with her mother and her brother. A writer with a novel and a collection of short stories already to her credit, Marty had recently returned from Germany, where she had collected information for a book on the Nazis.

Ernest was smitten and turned on his full charm as he showed the Gellhorns around Key West. When he took them home, instinct told Pauline at once that the girl with the long, honey-colored hair and the young figure was a threat and not just a passing infatuation. When Marty's mother and brother went home to St. Louis, she stayed on, spending most of her time with the Hemingways. She seemed to be equally interested in both Hemingways, but Pauline saw through the pretense. She had done the same thing years ago when she met Ernest and Hadley in Paris.

Ernest took Marty to Sloppy Joe's and other cafés, showing her off like a trophy. When Marty finally left Key West in mid-January of 1937, Pauline knew her marriage was in trouble.

Ernest, meanwhile, gave up hope of finishing the troublesome novel before going to Spain. In New York, he signed a contract with the North American Newpaper Alliance that set his pay at five hundred dollars for reports cabled from Spain and one thousand dollars for longer articles sent by mail. While in New York he helped with the script for a Loyalist propaganda film called *Spain in Flames*. Although Ernest had misgivings about the Loyalist cause and its fighting strategy, he greatly favored that side over the rebels who had already invited Moorish, Italian, and German invaders to Spanish soil. Rebel leader Francisco Franco was supported by the fascists, and Ernest was sure the war in Spain was a prelude to a much larger struggle against fascism.

Although he returned to Key West briefly, Ernest was back in New York in February in time to board the liner *Paris,*

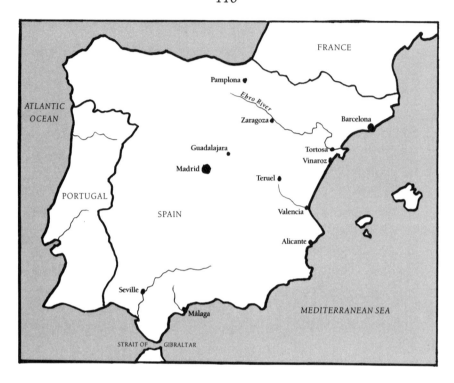

bound for France. Before sailing, he told reporters he was going to Spain to tell Americans about a new kind of war, a total war that involved both soldiers and civilians. His prediction proved true.

In Paris, the American State Department delayed issuing Sidney Franklin a visa to enter Spain. Ernest waited for ten days and then headed south alone in a chartered car. When French border guards told him his own visa would not allow him into Spain, Ernest drove to an airport and flew across the border without difficulty. He landed in Alicante on the southeast coast on March 16, 1937. In Valencia, several miles up the coast by car, the government press office gave Ernest credentials and provided a car and driver to take him to Madrid. Once there, he went straight to the censor's office and asked permission to visit Guadalajara, fifty miles to the northeast, where Loyalist forces had recently defeated three Italian divisions. General Hans Kahle, a German veteran of the world war who had fled from the Nazis, offered to guide Ernest to the battlefield.

During the drive, the two men became friends. Ernest was impressed with Kahle's confident manner, and Kahle was pleased to find a correspondent who spoke Spanish well, knew Spain, and understood military strategy.

Burials were still in progress when they arrived on the battlefield. Ernest was fascinated by abandoned machine guns, trucks, tanks, ammunition crates, and other smoking wreckage of a war. He looked at the terrain and reconstructed the battle with little help from Kahle.

Back in Madrid, although rebel shells exploded in the city daily, Ernest felt optimistic for an early Loyalist victory. As the fighting wore on, however, Loyalist mistakes and inefficiency repeatedly gave Franco's forces the advantage.

Ernest set up headquarters with other correspondents in the Hotel Florida in time to welcome Sidney Franklin and Marty Gellhorn to Madrid. Ernest, who was already acting as if he had military and government contacts in high places, angered Marty and several other correspondents with his superior manner. Ernest's remarkable charm and his fluent Spanish, however, gave him an advantage. He had indeed quickly gathered many valuable sources of information. Ernest wanted to serve as Marty's guide, but her independent nature soon rebelled. She wanted to prove herself without Ernest's help. She also thought Ernest had a distorted view of the war. She found him so fascinated with military tactics that he often failed to appreciate the more important political implications of the struggle.

Although usually by herself during the day, Marty spent most of her evenings with Ernest. The excitement of war and Marty's company soon dispelled all the depression that had built up during his struggle with the novel. He felt rejuvenated. The creative forces surged again.

Chapter 16

Dateline Madrid

DURING MOST OF APRIL 1937, ERNEST HELPED A CAMera crew get action shots for *The Spanish Earth,* another film designed to rouse public feelings and gain sympathy for the Loyalists. The world viewed Spain with ambivalence at this time. Volunteers from many Western nations had come to fight against fascism, but Western governments remained neutral. *The Spanish Earth,* it was hoped, would break down the neutrality.

Filming was difficult. Dust and smoke obscured the action, and the film crew could rarely get close enough for decent pictures. Soldiers looked like ants and tanks like small beetles.

On April 9 the camera crew found some abandoned apartment buildings outside of Madrid that gave a good view of a Loyalist offensive. Many of Ernest's fellow correspondents, including Marty and John Dos Passos, joined him there in time to see a tank attack fizzle.

This was one of the rare times when Marty and Ernest worked together during the day. She went off on her own so often and was usually so indifferent to Hemingway's advice and opinions that no one guessed for several weeks that she and Ernest had become lovers.

The truth came the night a rebel shell burst the hot water boiler and filled the Hotel Florida with steam. As the correspondents hurried for the stairs, Marty and Ernest were seen running out of the same bedroom.

John Dos Passos, meanwhile, had been searching several weeks for a lost friend. José Robles Pazos, Dos's Spanish translator, had been falsely arrested as a traitor by the Loyalists. The man was a hero in Dos's eyes, and many of his friends agreed. Even government officials said that Robles Pazos was sure to be released. No one wanted to admit that he had been executed soon after his arrest. When Ernest learned the truth and told about the tragedy in an offhand manner, Dos was outraged, and when Ernest added that Robles Pazos probably deserved to be shot, Dos withdrew his friendship with Hemingway.

Ernest had heroes of his own. He welcomed all the American volunteer pilots to his room and provided food and drink for them during their off-duty hours. He thought Colonel Gustavo Durán, an artist he first met in Paris, one of the bravest men he knew. General Hans Kahle, who now headed the Eleventh International Brigade, was another hero. Although Ernest visited the Eleventh often, his favorite outfit was the Twelfth Brigade commanded by a good-humored Hungarian who fought under the name of General Lucasz.

Ernest could detach himself easily from the war. One day he went hunting with a borrowed shotgun and returned to the Florida with a duck, a partridge, and four rabbits.

Although he thought until the final days that the Loyalists would win, he now knew that it would be a long and bloody struggle. He was so sure of this that he decided at the end of April to go home and finish his novel. Then he could think about returning to Spain. Marty also decided to spend most of the summer in the United States.

Ernest arrived in New York on May 18 and headed at once for Key West. There, he bustled his family aboard *Pilar* and sailed to Bimini, hoping to fish and write. The Harry Morgan novel was still troublesome, and his work was interrupted by several trips to the mainland. In New York early in June he spoke before the Second American Writers Congress, a strongly antifascist, pro-Communist group organized in large part by Donald Ogden Stewart and other friends. Many of them were later blacklisted in Hollywood as Communist sympathizers.

Ernest's speech was short, but his appearance on stage received an ovation. Most members of the enthusiastic audience mistakenly concluded that Hemingway had become politically involved at last.

Later in June, he returned to New York to help edit *The Spanish Earth*. The job was finished in time for a premiere showing at the White House early in July. Meanwhile, Ernest finally turned over the typescript for the Harry Morgan novel to Max Perkins. It was called *To Have and Have Not*.

A few days later, Ernest went to Hollywood to help raise money for Loyalist Spain. He spoke and showed *The Spanish Earth* to a select group of actors and directors who contributed twenty thousand dollars toward the purchase of ambulances. Scott Fitzgerald, who attended the meeting, said Ernest's sincerity bordered on religious zeal.

Ernest returned to Bimini in time to celebrate his thirty-eighth birthday. Soon after, however, he learned that Marty was returning to Spain, and so he brought his own vacation to an end.

In New York, a few days before sailing to France, Ernest went to Perkins's office and came face to face with Max Eastman, author of the "Bull in the Afternoon" article. Four years had passed since the article appeared, and Perkins hoped the meeting would be cordial. It was anything but. Ernest first unbuttoned his shirt to show that he had plenty of real chest hair. Then he opened Eastman's shirt to show a bare chest. The laughter that followed was suddenly broken when Ernest hit Eastman in the face with a book. Before Perkins could stop them, the two men fell to the floor wrestling. Perkins was unable to pull the men apart, but the fight ended abruptly when Ernest got to his feet laughing. He left the office smiling, his temper apparently restored.

The fight, however, continued the next day in the newspapers. Eastman told reporters he had beaten Ernest in a wrestling match. Ernest was quoted as saying that the critic fought like a woman and would have been hurt if Ernest had continued fighting. The verbal battle was still raging when Ernest sailed away on August 14.

Although the Loyalists had recaptured some provinces and partially lifted the siege of Madrid, Franco's forces by now held two-thirds of Spain, including all the Basque provinces. General Lucasz and several other heroes of the Twelfth Brigade had been killed.

Marty and Ernest were among the first American journalists to inspect the Zaragosa front, where the Loyalists had won a battle. They interviewed Major Robert Merriman, who, despite many wounds, had led the Fifteenth International Brigade in a crucial assault. Ernest added Merriman to his list of heroes.

During several days in the field, Ernest and Marty slept under the stars and cooked their food over an open fire. The first snows had fallen, a cold wind chilled them, and they often turned in hungry, but Marty did not complain. Her stamina and enthusiasm won Ernest's admiration.

Madrid was almost peaceful. Although some sectors of the city were still being hit, there were days when no rebel shells fell anywhere. In Hotel Florida, Ernest turned his room, well stocked with food and drink, into unofficial headquarters for a great variety of officers. He could usually get all the interviews he needed without leaving the hotel. He also conducted interviews at the nearby Chicote Bar. There, Ernest provided the drinks, and at least on one occasion a pretty girl for a lonely officer.

When a lull came in the fighting, Ernest decided to write a play. He had the prototypes for more than enough characters, and the action could all take place in his hotel room. He cast himself as Philip Rawlings, a correspondent working undercover as a counterspy. Rawlings's mistress in the room next to his was modeled on Marty Gellhorn. With little more to invent than tough, he-man dialogue for his characters, the writing went quickly.

The Fifth Column was finished in late October, and soon after Ernest let it be known that he was looking for a producer, Scribner's was besieged with phone calls. Perkins knew little about the play and could only advise callers to wait until Ernest came home.

Meanwhile, *To Have and Have Not,* with twenty-five thousand copies sold in the first three weeks of its release, was number four on the national best-seller list.

In mid-December, still recovering from a cold, Ernest was preparing to leave Spain when he learned of a surprise Loyalist drive on Teruel. He and two other men were among the first correspondents to enter the city. Several citizens, mistaking Ernest for an officer, asked what they should do. He advised them to stay indoors until the house-to-house fighting ended. The people, however, were eager to celebrate. They embraced Ernest and his companions. The wine flowed. People danced in the streets. Ernest reveled in his role as liberator.

Ernest and Marty celebrated Christmas Eve together in

Barcelona and then went to Paris. Pauline was waiting for them. She had decided on a last ditch effort to save her marriage, but it was too late. She and Ernest argued endlessly. She cried. She threatened to jump from their hotel balcony. Ernest became sullen and moody. He was still in a black mood on January 15, 1938, when he and Pauline sailed for home.

Back in Key West, he tried to bury himself in work, but relations with Pauline remained tense and the news from Spain was bad. For several days, he thought he might help the Loyalist cause more by staying home and writing articles than by going to the front. On March 17, however, Ernest flew to New York. Two days later he sailed for Europe.

When he reached Barcelona on April 1, the city had just been bombed. A few miles south, Franco's forces were driving toward the sea to cut Barcelona off from Valencia. When Ernest and another correspondent drove south toward the front, a rebel plane strafed the road. They jumped from their car and took cover in a ditch. A few miles farther on, they met refugees followed by retreating troops, tanks, and artillery. The Loyalists hoped to make a stand on the north bank of the Ebro, but the situation was confused. Ernest talked to Americans in the Washington-Lincoln Battalion who had swum across the river to avoid capture.

Meanwhile, south of the river, Tortosa was being bravely defended, but thirty miles farther south at Vinaroz, Franco's forces reached the Mediterranean. With German and Italian airplanes droning overhead, Ernest, Marty, and two other correspondents tried to approach Vinaroz, but rebel fire forced them back. The bridge at Tortosa had been bombed, leaving a shaky footbridge as their only escape. By some miracle the bridge stood up under the weight of their car and they returned safely to the north bank of the Ebro.

Despite the Loyalist losses, when the spring rains slowed Franco, there was a surge of optimism. Ernest himself still thought the Loyalists would eventually win. Meanwhile, his contract with the North American Newspaper Alliance ended and was not renewed. Ernest left Spain thinking his work as a war correspondent was over.

Chapter 17

Marty

ERNEST SAILED HOME UNSURE OF HIS DOMESTIC situation. Friends in New York told him that Pauline considered the marriage finished, but he went home as if nothing had changed.

Although his reception was cool, he soon settled into a routine. He wrote short stories set in besieged Madrid and articles about the war for *Ken,* a new magazine that paid Ernest one hundred dollars a week for anything he wanted to write.

Ernest wrote, among other things, that the U.S. State Department had blocked arms shipments to the Loyalists, and he continued to predict that the Loyalists would win. By now, however, he may have been trying to justify his departure from the war. He would not have it said that he left during a crisis. Nor did he want it known that he no longer had a contract to cover the war. The editor of the North American Newspaper Alliance had been unhappy with his work, complaining that many Hemingway dispatches duplicated the wire service reports. He had asked Ernest to limit his reports to human interest features, but Ernest angrily refused to renew his contract on those terms.

Later, when NANA asked him to cover the Joe Louis–
Max Schmeling fight in New York in June, Ernest refused and
instead wrote an article on the fight for *Ken*.

Meanwhile, he had misgivings about producing his play
The Fifth Column. When Perkins agreed to publish it in a big
volume to be called *The Fifth Column and the First Forty-nine
Stories,* Ernest went home to prepare manuscripts.

He was still working on the collection in August when
the heat made Key West almost unbearable. Ernest and Pauline,
still making an outward show of a happy marriage, agreed on
a vacation together at the L Bar T in Wyoming. Ernest scratched
his eye soon after the trip started and had to recuperate for
two days in a Florida hotel. They arrived at the ranch in a
downpour, but he went right to work on the foreword for his
new collection.

When he finished it on August 20 he felt restless. Spain
worried him. He missed Marty. Abruptly he left Pauline, drove
to New York, and booked passage for France. In Paris, reunited
with Marty, he revised the Madrid stories and began a new
novel set in Spain.

In October *The Fifth Column and the First Forty-nine Stories,*
a volume of almost six hundred pages, was received with mixed
reviews. Ernest's anger cooled only slightly when Perkins reported that six thousand copies of the book sold in the first
two weeks. Actually, the critics generally liked the stories more
than the play, endorsing Ernest's own misgivings as a
playwright, but he remained angry for several days.

Pauline had insisted that he stay clear of the fighting, but
on November 4, 1938, he defied her and returned to Spain.
He drove to the Ebro with friends. The Fifteenth Brigade still
held a bridgehead on the south side of the river, but a retreat
had begun when Ernest arrived. Just the same, he and other

reporters tried to cross the river in a rowboat. The current was about to carry them into the wreckage of a bridge when Ernest took up an oar and worked the boat clear. When he discovered that many of his old friends in the brigade were dead or missing, Ernest came to the reluctant conclusion that the Loyalists had lost the war.

This time Ernest left Spain, not to return again until well after World War II. Pauline was waiting for him in New York, but she returned to Key West soon after he arrived. Meanwhile, Ernest agreed to let the Theatre Guild rewrite *The Fifth Column* and split the royalties with him.

Back in Key West, he wrote and promptly sold to *Cosmopolitan* "Nobody Ever Dies." It is probably his most inept story. The tale of two lovers trying to escape the secret police is so sentimental and full of he-man heroics that it reads like a parody of Hemingway. Surprisingly, he was pleased with it.

He was less than pleased with the changes the Theatre Guild had made in *The Fifth Column* and rushed to New York early in 1939 to put things right. He said the guild's version should be called "The Four Ninety-five Column Marked Down from Five." Although casting was about to begin, Ernest wrote two new acts and made several revisions which the guild patiently accepted.

Back in Key West, he toyed with the idea of writing the story Gutiérrez had told him about the Cuban fisherman and sharks, but it was so powerful that he did not feel ready to tackle it. Instead, he suggested a collection of his Spanish stories. Perkins liked the idea and Ernest went to Cuba in February to get to work.

He quickly finished three new stories to add to those that had already appeared in magazines. On March 1, he made a fresh start on the Spanish novel that he had begun in Paris the previous autumn. He wrote in his room in the Ambos

Mundos Hotel through the mornings and either fished or played tennis in the afternoons.

During the spring vacation, he went back to Key West briefly to see Bumby, but the house on Whitehead Street was so full of Pauline's friends that he found it difficult to write. When he returned to Cuba on April 10, he took up the new book with fresh enthusiasm. He thought it might be the best thing he had written yet.

He had promised Marty Gellhorn to look for a house they could rent, but the book took all his attention. When she came to Havana, she took on the house search herself. She quickly located the Finca Vigía, or View Farm, an old estate in San Francisco de Paula, a small village fifteen miles from Havana. It was a rambling house in need of much repair, surrounded by an unkept garden and a forest of tropical trees. Marty, however, promised to make it livable, and when Ernest heard that it could be had for one hundred dollars a month, he agreed to move in. The Finca would be his home for many years to come.

Once settled in the hilltop retreat, Ernest turned out seven hundred to a thousand words a day. Sometimes enthusiasm for his story kept him going far into the afternoon. The book grew beyond expectations. He thought he might finish in August. August came with seventy-six thousand words in rough draft, but the end was not in sight. He decided on a Wyoming vacation.

Pauline was in Europe with friends. The boys were in summer camp. Marty wanted to visit her mother in St. Louis. En route to the Norquist ranch, Ernest stopped at a guest ranch near Cody, Wyoming, where Hadley and her husband, Paul Mowrer, were vacationing. They had a cordial visit, talking mostly about Bumby.

From there Ernest continued to the L Bar T, arriving just

as news came over the radio of declaration of general war in Europe. Worried about Pauline, Ernest stayed up most of the night listening to the radio. Within a few days Pauline telephoned from New York to report her safe return and her plans to come to the ranch. Ernest was determined by now to end the marriage, but when Pauline arrived she had such a bad cold that a serious talk was out of the question. Ernest was still nursing her back to health when the boys arrived from their summer camps.

Ernest waited until she had fully recovered. Then he packed up the Ford and headed west alone.

Marty agreed by phone to meet him in Sun Valley, Idaho. The resort, built by the Union Pacific Railroad near the mining town of Ketchum, lies on the southern slope of the Sawtooth Mountains. It has superb skiing in the winter and excellent hunting and fishing in the summer. When Ernest and Marty first visited it, Sun Valley was still undiscovered. They had no trouble, their first night, in booking the most luxurious suite in the lodge.

Next day, Ernest at once made friends with the staff. Taylor Williams was a veteran guide full of hunting lore and good sense. Gene Van Guilder, who handled the resort publicity, was an enthusiastic outdoorsman. Tillie and Lloyd Arnold became his favorite couple. Lloyd was the lodge photographer, and Tillie had a talent for cooking game birds that won Ernest's heart.

Ernest wrote mornings and hunted or fished with one of his new friends in the afternoons, but tragedy soon shattered the routine. A shotgun, carelessly stowed in a canoe, went off, killing Van Guilder instantly. Ernest was deeply moved and wrote a eulogy which he read at the grave in Ketchum's small cemetery. It was difficult afterward to get back to work.

Meanwhile, Marty grew restless. With war raging in Europe and Asia, she was eager to pursue her career as a correspondent. She had asked *Collier's* magazine to send her to Finland, which had recently been invaded by Russia, and soon after Van Guilder's funeral, her application was approved.

Left alone, Ernest promptly turned his lodge suite into a gambling den. It became crowded with guests and staff members who played cards or shook dice far into the night. Somehow, he continued to rise early to write and had enough energy for hunting or fishing in the afternoon. He needed help with his correspondence, however, and enlisted Clara Spiegel, a friend of Van Guilder's widow, who came out from Chicago after the funeral, to take dictation. On one busy day he dictated fifty letters, and Clara typed them all without complaint. The two became good friends and one night talked at length about suicide. He also had long talks with the Arnolds. Once, when he described his mother as a bitch, Tillie scolded him severely.

Ernest wanted to spend Christmas in Key West with Pauline and the boys. Pauline, however, had started divorce proceedings and told him not to come. When he went anyway, Pauline took the boys to New York for the holidays. Ernest went on to Cuba, installed himself alone in the Finca, and worked on the novel.

He was working with more enthusiasm than ever when Marty returned from her assignment in Finland. Cuba, meanwhile, had become a haven for many Spanish exiles, including a community of Basques who had brought with them jai alai, their swift handball-style game that was ideal for betting. Marty and Ernest often played tennis with the Basques in the afternoons and went to a club to see them play jai alai at least one evening a week. Ernest also joined a gun club that shot live pigeons for its chief diversion. Later he bought some cocks and joined a cockfighting club.

His novel was still far from finished when he decided to

call it *For Whom the Bell Tolls,* a phrase from a poem by the seventeenth century Englishman John Donne. Donne's description of a funeral focuses on the idea that no one stands alone in life or in death. Ernest decided that the idea suited the Spanish tragedy perfectly.

As usual, he used many friends as prototypes for his characters. His hero, Robert Jordan, was a mirror image of Ernest himself. Jordan's midwestern parents were like his own. Jordan's father had even killed himself with a pistol.

On July 1, 1940, after completing the forty-third chapter, Ernest decided the story had been told. He left Jordan hiding under a tree waiting for a hero's death at the hands of an advancing Fascist patrol. It was a romantic ending for what Ernest presented as a highly realistic portrayal of the Spanish civil war.

Chapter 18

For Whom the Bell Tolls

ERNEST WIRED PERKINS THAT THE BOOK WAS FINISHED and went into downtown Havana to get his shaggy hair cut. Several weeks earlier he had vowed to remain unshorn and unshaven until the novel was finished. He came out of the barbershop feeling refreshed and ready for fun. His long struggle, however, had left him more exhausted mentally than ever before. He was also momentarily forgetful.

When he met a friend, the two went off to have a chat over drinks and lunch. When Marty found him in a bar at 4:00 P.M., she angrily reminded him that he had promised to take her to lunch. Ernest apologized, but Marty's patience had been badly strained.

Next day, deciding his story was not finished after all, Ernest began work on another chapter. A few days after it was finished, however, he decided the addition was not necessary.

When his typist finished the manuscript, Ernest took it to New York and delivered it to Perkins by hand. He returned to Cuba emotionally drained. He hoped a few weeks of fishing would revive him. Perkins, however, was eager to get the new novel into print. When the galley proofs arrived at the Finca,

Ernest had to get back to work. He was still checking proofs when Perkins sent news that the Book of the Month Club had selected *For Whom the Bell Tolls* for October release with a special printing of one hundred thousand copies. Scribner's itself planned a first printing of one hundred thousand for the regular trade market.

Ernest, who had been at work almost steadily for a year and a half, was too tired to appreciate the news fully. He took Marty and his sons to Sun Valley. Soon after settling into the lodge, he dedicated the book to Marty, sent off the final proof sheet, and got drunk.

Actually, he had been drinking heavily for several months, but because of his remarkable resilience, he almost always woke alert and eager for a productive morning of work. Now, with the work done, his drinking increased. Gradually it began to take a toll on his health and his talent.

His enthusiasm for the outdoors, however, remained high. Soon after Bumby left for his fall term of school, Ernest organized a Hemingway jackrabbit hunt. He, Marty, and the two younger boys returned with 320 rabbits after a day of shooting. Later, after all the boys had left, Ernest and Marty took a week-long camping trip into a wild region of the Middle Fork of the Salmon River.

When unusually heavy rains kept him indoors, Ernest made friends with other guests, including Gary Cooper, who had played Lieutenant Henry in *A Farewell to Arms*. Although Ernest had not liked the movie, he liked Cooper, and began thinking of him in the role of Robert Jordan, hero of *For Whom the Bell Tolls*. This was not an idle thought. Donald Friede, whom Ernest had recently hired as his Hollywood agent, soon sold film rights to Paramount Pictures for a record $136,000, and Cooper did play the hero's role.

Meanwhile, reviews of the book itself were the best Hemingway had ever received. It was "rare and beautiful," a combination of "strength and brutality," one rave declared. The love scenes, said another critic, were the best in American fiction. The consensus was that a mature Hemingway had produced the best book of his career. Meanwhile, the Book of the Month Club doubled its printing order to 200,000 books, and Scribner's added 160,000 to its initial order of 100,000.

Marty was pleased for Ernest, but she was also deeply concerned about world events. Before leaving Sun Valley, she arranged to go to war-ravaged China for *Collier's* magazine. Ernest planned to go with her. The Chinese had been fighting each other since 1928 and fighting Japanese invaders since 1931.

Marty and Ernest were still in Idaho when his divorce from Pauline became final. Ernest had not contested the charge of desertion, and Pauline received custody of Patrick and Gregory. The marriage had lasted thirteen years. He remained single three weeks.

On November 21, 1940, soon after starting their drive east, Ernest and Marty were married by a justice of the peace in Cheyenne, Wyoming. After the simple ceremony, they continued to New York, where Ernest signed a contract with *PM,* a new tabloid, to write six articles on China. The Hemingways then went to Cuba for the holidays. The trip to China would begin late in January.

Meanwhile, they bought the Finca, paying $12,500 for the hilltop estate soon after Christmas. They were busy making plans for improvements when the sad news came of Scott Fitzgerald's death of a heart attack. Although his friendship with Scott had deteriorated, Ernest remembered their early years in Paris with much warmth.

He was still in a nostalgic mood when he learned that Margaret Anderson, a magazine editor he had known in Paris, was penniless in France and unable to escape the Nazis. He immediately sent four hundred dollars for her passage to the United States.

The Hemingways went to New York in late January and caught a flight for Los Angeles. Gary Cooper met their plane and told them Ingrid Bergman was interested in playing Maria, the heroine in *For Whom the Bell Tolls*. Ernest met her for lunch and approved. Then he and Marty sailed for Hawaii. In Honolulu, Ernest reluctantly agreed to speak to a group of English students from the University of Hawaii. He did not like the academic climate of the meeting and he was distressed to discover that no liquor would be served. He filled his talk with bad grammar and faulty pronunciations and concluded by saying that *A Farewell to Arms* was an immoral book, knowing very well that this was the best way to excite student interest in it. That evening at a party in his honor, a drunken Ernest almost got in a fight with another guest. Hawaii did not see the best of Hemingway.

When Marty and Ernest arrived in the British Crown colony of Hong Kong, they put up for a month's stay in a plush suite of the Repulse Bay Hotel. Here there was little evidence of war. The shops were crowded, the streets were festive, food was excellent and plentiful. Fans crowded to the racetrack every afternoon.

Early in March, however, Ernest and Marty went by air and car to Shaokwan, headquarters of the Seventh war zone, and got a taste of the fighting. They saw Generalissimo Chiang Kai-shek's regulars entrenched against the Japanese. Conditions were primitive. Military fare included a rice wine that was flavored with small snakes coiled in the bottom of each

Officers welcome Ernest and Martha near the front during their tour of China in 1941. (Hemingway Society)

bottle. Marty could not drink it, but Ernest smacked his lips and tried to persuade her to sample another variety that had small birds in the dregs.

When officers gave them a walking tour of the front, Ernest was full of enthusiasm, but Marty, suffering from the cold and filth and a persistent fungus infection, yearned for civilized comfort. She had to wait. From Shaokwan, they went down the North River by sampan and rode ponies through country where the rain never stopped. Finally, in April, they flew to Chungking, the wartime capital of China, where a hotel offered such luxuries as a warm bath and room service.

After they interviewed Generalissimo Chiang Kai-shek, with Madame Chiang serving as interpreter, Ernest concluded that Chiang was a better military leader than statesman. But

China itself impressed Ernest. He inspected a modern officers' training school with approval. He was awed by the sight of huge gangs building a landing field without machines. The Chinese, he concluded, were capable of just about anything.

In mid-April, Ernest and Martha left China by flying to Lashio, the southern end of the seven-hundred-mile Burma Road, which had been built to bring supplies into besieged China. From there they drove to Rangoon, where Martha flew to Jakarta to report on the political situation in Indonesia while Ernest went to Hong Kong to rest before starting the long flight home.

He crossed the Pacific in a flying clipper that was delayed so often by storms it took nearly a month to reach America. When he arrived in New York, he turned in the first of his articles to *PM* and waited for Marty. Sales of *For Whom the Bell Tolls* were climbing at record pace toward the five hundred thousand mark, but Ernest learned to his dismay that the book's nomination for a Pulitzer Prize had been vetoed by Columbia University president Nicholas Murray Butler, chairman of the Pulitzer advisory board. The news gave him further reason to dislike the academic world.

The trip to China had left him tired. He had no desire to write. His spirits fell so low that he began to see the marriage to Marty as a mistake. Marty was the first of his wives to have a career, and it often seemed to conflict with their marriage. She was also more independent than his previous wives. She proved this soon after they returned to Cuba. When cruising on *Pilar,* it was not unusual for Marty to jump ship if she was not having a good time. She would simply get off the boat at the first convenient port and find a ride back to the Finca. Ernest, who had never been confronted with mutiny, was stunned.

They usually remained on good terms, however, and both found pleasure in entertaining guests at the Finca. Members of the American embassy staff were frequent evening visitors. Robert P. Joyce, one of the first secretaries, and his wife, Jane, and Ellis O. Briggs, the ranking officer, became close friends of the Hemingways. Ernest was an excellent host, providing stimulating conversation as well as good food, vintage wine, and abundant liquor. He was witty, entertaining, and extremely sensitive to the needs of his guest. If there was an argument brewing, Ernest could sense it at once and divert the antagonists. Briggs described Ernest as the most perceptive person he knew.

He wrote very little during 1941, but he had abundant energy. Late in September, soon after a return trip to Sun Valley, he organized an antelope hunt. With Taylor Williams as guide, Ernest took Bumby, Patrick, and Gregory to a remote valley, east of Ketchum. After they cornered a herd in a box canyon, Ernest performed the most remarkable feat of marksmanship Williams had ever seen. The instant Ernest saw the herd run, he jumped from his saddle, rifle in hand, and ran to a vantage point. He threw himself prone and fired, all in one motion, and the largest buck in the herd fell dead.

After the boys returned to school, Marty and Ernest remained at Sun Valley until early December. It was during their drive east that they heard of the Japanese attack on Pearl Harbor. Shocked and angry, the Hemingways wanted to go to work at once as correspondents, but the military situation remained too confused for several months to allow correspondents in the field.

With war raging, Ernest could not bring himself to write fiction. He agreed, however, to write a preface and help select war stories and articles for a collection planned by Crown Publishers. He thought the book, to be called *Men at War,* might lift morale.

Meanwhile, he began planning a personal campaign against the enemy.

Chapter 19

War Again

ERNEST PERSUADED HIS FRIENDS IN THE EMBASSY TO let him set up his own counterintelligence organization. It had long been rumored that Nazi agents, taking advantage of anti-American sentiment in Cuba, collected information on Allied shipping and passed it on to the U-boats that sometimes patrolled Caribbean waters.

Although the rumors were exaggerations, they seemed very threatening at the time, and Ernest quickly built a network of agents. Drawn from his wide circle of friends, the agents included bartenders, waiters, fishermen, jai alai players, panhandlers, and one Catholic priest. Although they called themselves the "Crook Factory," they took their work seriously.

The Finca, much to Marty's dismay, served as headquarters. Counterspies stepped out of the shadows at any hour, day or night, asking for "Ernesto" to present to him their reports. The operation was loose. Some spies wrote their findings, others whispered them to the boss. The hush-hush business was often concluded with drinks on the veranda. Later, Ernest typed up the reports and delivered them to his friends at the embassy.

Once the Crook Factory was well launched, Ernest searched for another way to help win the war. He found it while reading selections for *Men at War*. During World War I, Count Felix von Luckner had disguised his German raider, or Q-boat, as an innocent fishing boat. When patrols stopped him, Luckner uncovered his guns and captured or sank the British vessels. As soon as Ernest read about von Luckner, he began to see *Pilar* as the ideal Q-boat.

It was a wild idea, but a few Cuban fishermen had been stopped by U-Boats. German sailors boarded and took fresh food and sometimes water. Ernest took his plan to the embassy. He convinced his friends that with enough guns and hand-thrown bombs aboard, he could sink any German submarine that tried to stop *Pilar*. If *Pilar* were stopped, his strategy would be to wait until the German boarding party appeared on the U-boat's deck. Then he would speed to within twenty yards and begin throwing bombs and shooting. U.S. naval experts had serious misgivings about the scheme, but the embassy unofficially endorsed it and provided most of the bazookas, bombs, grenades, and machine guns that Ernest requested. He gathered a crew of eight men, loaded the arms under cover of night, and began running regular patrols in June.

Nothing happened. In many months of cruising, Ernest and his men spotted just one submarine and it was dropping out of sight over the horizon. Just the same, Ernest took the work seriously. Marty did not. She once accused him of inventing the whole operation simply to make sure he would be supplied with rationed fuel. The accusation sent Ernest into a rage.

Meanwhile, Marty, an orderly person by nature, could bring no order to the Finca. Ernest had no regular schedule. He and the crew of *Pilar* could appear unshaven, dirty, tired, hungry, and thirsty at any time. Ernest might fall into bed or stay up all night drinking with his men. And then there was the Finca's great gang of cats that Ernest had allowed to breed uncontrolled and failed to house-train. They outraged Marty and made walking from room to room a hazardous adventure.

Ernest showed little sympathy. He made fun of her career and criticized her writing. She began to travel. She went to St. Louis to see her mother. Then she toured the Caribbean to get material for a war-readiness report on the area for *Collier's*. She hiked in the jungles of Dutch Guiana. She took a cruise on a chartered yacht. She went to Washington, D.C., to visit friends.

Ernest, now wearing a full beard, drank more than ever. His Sunday evening friends were amazed at his ability to drink so much without showing any ill effects. He started a typical evening with absinthe before dinner, red and white wine plus champagne during the meal, and several Scotch highballs after dinner. Although he appeared sober, Ernest confessed that hangovers sometimes made it impossible for him to write. But other than letters to friends, he was still doing very little writing. When *Men at War* was published to mixed reviews, however, he decided it was time to resume his career.

In November 1942, he persuaded Gustavo Durán, one of his heroes in the Spanish civil war who had recently arrived in Cuba, to take charge of the Crook Factory. Durán, however, soon found more important work in the United States Embassy and neglected espionage. Ernest was again enraged.

Meanwhile, Marty came home from her travels to write a novel. The Hemingways quarreled frequently. Ernest's childish petulance was often at odds with his he-man image. One evening, after scolding Marty in a Havana restaurant for not buying more expensive gifts for their servants, Ernest left her to find her way home by herself. After another Havana evening, when Marty insisted on driving because he was far from sober, Ernest struck her with the back of his hand. Marty deliberately turned off the road and crunched the car slowly into a tree. The Hemingways walked home separately.

Ernest began spending afternoons at the bar in Havana's Hotel Floridita. He encouraged his many friends there to call him "Papa." And to add further glow to his self-image, he told imaginative tales about his war exploits in Italy. There were times, however, when his self-image darkened and he told friends he was finished with writing.

As 1943 dawned, the war seemed to come closer. Many of Ernest's friends were joining the service. Bumby left Dartmouth College to go to officers' training school, preparing for duty in the military police. Marty, bringing her novel to a close, made plans to go to London for *Collier's*. She urged Ernest to get involved, but he continued to take *Pilar* out on unproductive patrols.

A few weeks after Ernest's forty-fourth birthday, Marty left for London. When Patrick and Gregory went back to school, Ernest found himself alone with his cats and the servants. He began staying on patrol for several days at a time. He became morose and full of self-pity, complaining bitterly of his loneliness and his inability to write. Although he talked about going to England, he did nothing about it.

He might have remained in Cuba for the duration, had not Marty come to the rescue. The Royal Air Force had begun sending its bombers on daring, daylight missions over Germany. Marty persuaded her friends at *Collier's* to ask Ernest to cover the story. To her delight, he agreed and arrived in London on May 18, 1944.

He was a celebrity and his arrival was news. He immediately began receiving reporters in his room in the lavish Hotel Dorchester. His room was also a gathering place for friends. Gregory Clark from the *Toronto Star*, Lewis Galantière from the early days in Paris, and Robert Capa, a photographer he had known in Spain, were among those who came to see him. Ernest's brother, Leicester Hemingway, who was working with a documentary film crew, dropped in frequently. Ernest played host to what seemed a continuous party.

Marty was away when Ernest arrived in London, and scores of women were eager to meet the great author. Mary Welsh, who worked for *Time*, *Life*, and *Fortune* magazines, was an ardent admirer. Ernest was enchanted by the petite blond. Eight years younger than Ernest, with a high level of intelligence and enthusiasm, Mary was pleased by Ernest's attention and charmed by his enthusiasm. Her husband, Noel Monks, was frequently out of town on assignment for the *Daily Mail*.

Because of a car accident, Ernest's work with the RAF had to be postponed. It happened in the early hours of May 25 after an evening of heavy drinking. Ernest was riding home in a friend's car when the driver, who could see very little in the blacked-out city, ran head-on into a steel water tank. Ernest's head broke the windshield. His knees smashed the dashboard. He was pulled dazed from the car with blood streaming from a deep scalp wound.

Doctors at St. George's Hospital closed the wound with fifty-seven stitches and sent Ernest to the London Clinic to convalesce from a severe concussion. He was still bedridden when Marty arrived in London. When she learned he had been hurt in the aftermath of a party, she gave him little sympathy. It was time, she said, to start taking the war seriously. He agreed.

Allied landings in Europe were expected to begin soon,

and Ernest feared he might miss them. Meanwhile, as soon as he had recovered enough to return to the Dorchester, he rescheduled the RAF assignment. He was promised some flights in June. He was suffering severe headaches and doctors told him not to drink, but Ernest continued to appear almost nightly with friends in taverns or bars, drinking heavily. He was not universally popular. One RAF officer observed that Ernest seemed to be playing the part of Hemingway and not doing a very convincing job. The invasion of France finally ended his party.

On June 2, Ernest and hundreds of other correspondents were briefed and then taken to the south coast of England, where the biggest assault fleet in history was massed. On the night of June 5, with head aching and knees still sore, Ernest boarded an attack transport that soon headed toward Normandy. At dawn, he climbed down the rope netting hung on the side of the ship to enter a landing craft. The little boat, jammed with pale-faced soldiers, headed for the beach as fourteen-inch navy shells screamed overhead. Using his hunting binoculars, Ernest tried to see the shoreline, but the boat pitched too violently to bring anything into focus. As they drew closer, however, wreckage of earlier assault waves loomed out of the battle haze. Smoke poured from two tanks mired in the sand. Bodies of the dead rolled in the surf. A landing craft nearby foundered in the waves.

Ernest marveled at the daring of destroyer captains who ran their ships within yards of the beach to fire five-inch guns point blank at German bunkers. The thunder of explosion and gunfire was constant. He was surrounded by smoke and flame.

When his craft grounded on the beach, the forward ramp banged down and the soldiers waded out. Ernest stayed aboard as the craft backed off to return to the assault vessel for more men. Ernest climbed aboard the bigger craft. The adventure had been brief, but it was his first exposure to danger since the Spanish civil war, and it sobered him.

Back at the Dorchester, he at once began writing his dispatch on the invasion. Marty, who had actually landed on a beachhead briefly, returned to London with the news that she would soon leave to cover the Italian front. She told Ernest she had come to cover the war, not live at the Dorchester. Ernest was now eager to work too.

He wrote about the German buzz bombs that had begun raising havoc in London. Then his flights with the RAF began. The RAF Typhoon could intercept a 400-mile-an-hour buzz bomb and sometimes shoot one down. Ernest interviewed some of the pilots who had made "kills." Then he flew in a Mitchell medium bomber as it attacked a buzz bomb lauching site. During the bomb run, one of the twelve planes in his squadron was shot down by antiaircraft fire.

Toward the end of June, he went up twice in the rear seat of a Mosquito fighter. Mosquito pilots flew day and night to attack German supply lines behind the Normandy beach-heads. Although Ernest's pilot did not take him over France, he did try to intercept a buzz bomb on the second flight. The fighter was too slow for a clear shot, but Ernest thought just the same that they may have downed one of the rockets. He was so excited after this experience that he stayed up all night talking to Mosquito pilots. Some of them had been in combat more than four years. Ernest felt he was among heroes again. That morning, instead of going to bed, Ernest began writing his dispatch.

His spirits had not been so high for years.

Chapter 20

With the Infantry

WHEN HIS RAF ASSIGNMENT ENDED, ERNEST CROSSED the English Channel in a light plane to join two fellow correspondents who had taken over a villa in Cherbourg. Before leaving England, he had shaved off his beard. Perhaps he simply wanted to look more like a correspondent and less like a Caribbean pirate, but he was putting two wasted years behind him. Shaving the beard may have been a symbolic act.

Ernest returned to London long enough for a farewell lunch with Mary Welsh; then, on July 18, he returned to France and soon joined the press corps attached to the Fourth Infantry Division. It would be a long association.

The division was about to start a drive against tough German resistance. During the press briefing, Ernest met several officers, including Colonel Charles "Buck" Lanham, commander of the Twenty-second Regiment. Short, tough, and highly professional, Lanham had little time for correspondents, but Ernest's military knowledge, sensible questions, and command of French made a good first impression.

Ernest followed the Twenty-second Regiment for nine dusty days across low Normandy hills that were strewn with burned-out tanks, captured guns, and German and Allied dead. It was exhilarating. He was up before dawn every day. Sometimes he forgot to eat.

On July 31, at Villebaudon, he acquired two vehicles, a motorcycle with a sidecar and a Mercedes-Benz convertible. The driver assigned to him repaired and repainted the car, but Ernest preferred the motorcycle. When he and the driver roared into Villedieu-les-Poêles on August 1, the sidecar was well stocked with hand grenades.

The villagers thought he was an officer and led him to a house where they said several Germans were sheltered in the cellar. Ernest shouted in both German and French for the men to surrender. Then he tossed three grenades into the cellar. The action violated his noncombatant status as a correspondent, but Ernest's enthusiasm blinded him to rules. The cellar, he said later, was probably empty. Before he could investigate, the town mayor embraced Ernest and gave him two bottles of champagne. A few moments later, Ernest surrendered one of the bottles to Colonel Lanham, who was passing through town on his way to regimental headquarters.

Two days later, Ernest was trying to find the headquarters when he almost ran into a German antitank gun. He and the driver jumped into a ditch as the gun crew opened fire with machine guns. Two tense hours in hiding followed before the Germans finally withdrew.

In his daily letters to Mary Welsh, Ernest shamelessly exaggerated his exploits. He said the Fourth Division counted on him for reconnaissance, that the general gave him guns and ammunition, and that he had been knocked down by a shell fired from a German tank. Despite his lies, one truth was clear: He was having a wonderful time.

His dispatches for *Collier's* also contained many inaccu-

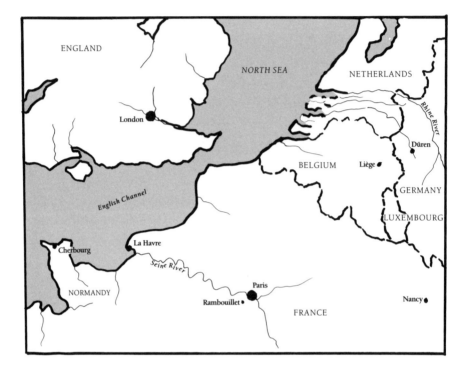

racies. As he had done in Spain, he often wrote as if he were covering the war by himself. He invented dialogue. He took secondhand information and turned it into a personal experience without always checking it out; but he captured the atmosphere and feel of the fighting with so much accuracy that it was almost uncanny.

Some of his friends thought Hemingway had a sixth sense. Lanham was convinced of this after Ernest refused to attend a regimental party in a Norman castle. He said the place made him uncomfortable. Next day, the Germans launched a counterattack. The castle was shelled, and several of Lanham's officers were killed. Lanham himself was slightly wounded.

Ernest soon actually did begin serving as advance scout for the regiment. His knowledge of languages and the French people did indeed lead him to information on German positions, and he was quick to evaluate the strategic importance of those positions. His news dispatches became secondary to scouting. As a noncombatant, however, his intelligence work had to remain unofficial.

When it became clear that Paris would be liberated before summer's end, Ernest tried to discover which units would reach the city first. He had to be with them. On August 21, after passing through Chartres, he tried to find the advanced members of the Fifth Infantry Division, who were thought to be on the road to Paris. Ernest and his driver fell in behind two truckloads of French partisans.

Near Rambouillet, thirty miles west of Paris, the little column stopped before a heavily mined German roadblock. While a U.S. Army lieutenant disarmed the mines, the French irregulars donned U.S. Army uniforms found in an abandoned truck and followed Ernest into Rambouillet on foot. When Ernest learned from the villagers that eight hundred Germans with fifteen tanks were poised to retake the town, he began organizing a hasty defense.

He sent the French partisans out on regular patrols. He integrated a detachment from the Fifth Infantry Division into his little corps. He persuaded division supply officers to send up arms and ammunition for his Frenchmen. He set up a command post and arsenal in a three-story hotel that, by happy chance, had a well-stocked wine cellar. Ernest interviewed villagers and received reports from his men like a veteran officer.

When David Bruce, an army secret service colonel, arrived, he persuaded the division to send up thirty more men.

That night, the defenders of Rambouillet traded shots with a German patrol. Next day, several correspondents arrived with the news that the Second French Armored Division under General Jacques Leclerc had been named to spearhead the liberation of Paris. Leclerc was expected in Rambouillet at any moment. Leclerc, however, was an extremely cautious officer.

Meanwhile, Ernest learned from French citizens just returned from Paris that the road lay virtually undefended. He soon knew the positions of those few Germans who remained along the route. As a political gesture, however, the Allies had to wait for Leclerc. Ernest fumed over the delay. When Leclerc's advance patrols finally arrived, they would not take Ernest's directions. Just east of town, the French patrols ran into a German ambush and were driven back with two killed and two wounded.

While the patrols were regrouping, Leclerc himself arrived. He had the good sense to listen to the information that Ernest had gathered, and the advance on Paris finally began. Ernest and David Bruce, with an army driver at the wheel, rode a jeep in the center of the column.

Although several roadblocks had to be cleared, Leclerc met no serious resistance, and reached the outskirts of Paris at 5:00 P.M., August 24. The citizens, wild with joy, greeted every Allied solder with tears and laughter, hugs and kisses, wine and flowers. The tricolor flew from almost every window. Soldiers and civilians shouted *"Vive la France"* until everyone was hoarse.

Rifles cracked and cannons boomed in the center of the city, which was still held by Germans. Fighting continued the next day as Leclerc slowly advanced. The column stopped again and again. Early in the afternoon, not far from the Bois de Boulogne, a shell fired from a German-occupied house exploded in their path. While soldiers took cover behind buildings and trees, Ernest, with carbine at the ready, ushered fellow correspondents out of the line of fire and made them wait until a French tank destroyed the German house.

Later in the afternoon, Ernest left the slow column. He was able to direct his driver down side streets to skirt around three German tanks that had blocked the main route. Thanks to the maneuver, Bruce and Ernest were among the first to reach the Arc de Triomphe. They climbed to the top for a view of the city. Flames flickered from several buildings. Smoke billowed from a vehicle at the far end of the Champs-Elysées. A tank burned beyond in the Tuileries Gardens. Sniper fire cracked all around them.

Later, after a high-speed drive on the deserted Champs-Elysées, they stopped at the Travelers Club, where the elderly club president opened champagne to celebrate the appearance of the first Americans since the occupation. They next went to the Ritz Hotel, found it open and undamaged, and rented rooms. Soon after Ernest and Bruce ordered fifty martinis, Ernest decided that the Ritz would be his headquarters for the rest of his stay in Paris. Hemingway parties for officers and fellow journalists soon began.

French newspapers described Ernest as a hero of the liberation. He told reporters he was amazed to find so little changed since his early days in Paris. News cameras captured his joyful reunion with Sylvia Beach. When Mary Welsh arrived at the Ritz, Ernest hugged her and swung her off her feet with glee.

While Ernest held court at the Ritz, Buck Lanham's regiment had been part of a northern drive that forced the Germans back to the Belgian border. When he sent a note telling Ernest he had missed some good action, Ernest reacted recklessly. On September 2, with little preparation and poor knowl-

lessly. On September 2, with little preparation and poor knowledge of the route, Ernest left Paris to find Lanham's outfit. He took one of the French partisans with him as driver.

The rapid Allied advance had bypassed pockets of German troops, some heavily armed. The roadways were strewn with debris. They had to stop again and again to fix punctures. Detours around blown bridges and mop-up battles delayed them. They were lucky to get through safely, and the effort proved futile. When Ernest finally arrived at Lanham's headquarters, the regiment was getting ready to relocate. Military plans were uncertain. Ernest promised to join the regiment later and drove back to Paris.

Ernest returned to the front on September 10. Lanham's regiment was fighting in hilly forests west of Liège, some eighty miles inside Belgium. Ernest was in a jocular mood. Once, while he and Lanham waited for the repair of a bridge, a villager asked him how he could live so long without becoming a general. Ernest replied with a straight face and a woeful sigh that he had never learned to read and write.

On September 12, Ernest watched the first American tanks cross the border into Germany. That evening he slept on German soil. His new home was an abandoned farmhouse. As soon as he woke, he began putting the place in order. He fed the cat and dog, sent off for some villagers to milk the cows, shot two chickens, rounded up some vegetables, salad greens, wine, and whiskey, and invited Buck Lanham and several journalists to dinner. Lanham later described it as his happiest night of the war.

Bloody fighting, however, lay ahead. The Germans, now defending their homeland, had the advantage of high ground and well-entrenched defenses. Ernest was eager for the battle to begin.

Chapter 21

Mary

IN MID-SEPTEMBER, WHEN THE ALLIES LAUNCHED THE first assault on the concrete bunkers, hidden guns, and mine fields on Germany's western border, Ernest was in bed in regimental headquarters with a bad cold. He returned to the front as soon as possible, however, and learned that German defenses had been broken at terrible cost. Lanham lost sixty-five men in one day.

After Ernest interviewed enough men to file an eyewitness report of the battle, he relocated his headquarters in another abandoned farmhouse. He stocked it with food, wine, and hand grenades. By now a legend in the regiment, he frequently entertained journalists who had come to interview him. He always sent them away with many Hemingway stories. He often did not need to exaggerate his exploits.

One evening while Ernest was entertaining Lanham and several other friends, a German artillery shell crashed through the farmhouse without exploding. Lanham ordered everyone into the cellar, but Ernest would not leave the table. While Lanham argued with him, another shell crashed through one wall and out the other. Ernest sipped his wine and cut his

Ernest and Buck Lanham at the front (Hemingway Society and Buck Lanham)

steak. Lanham gave up and sat down to enjoy his own meal. Another shell went through the building before the barrage stopped and the other guests returned to the table.

Thanks to a few jealous journalists, Ernest's military activities at Rambouillet had come to the attention of the attorney general's office. He was summoned to answer charges in October. Ernest feared that he might be stripped of his credentials and sent home in disgrace.

The inspector was stationed in Nancy, and when Ernest arrived there, he had made up his mind to bluff his way through the interview. It worked. He said he may have removed his jacket with the correspondent insignia briefly, but only because of the heat. He admitted going on patrol with partisans, but it was only to gather information. He never led any patrols. Frenchmen who called him colonel or general did so only out of respect. He said the arms stored in his rooms were there only as a convenience for the brave partisans.

It did not sound very convincing, but so many other correspondents and army officers were eager to testify in Hemingway's defense that the charges were dropped. Ernest hurried to Paris, the comfort of the Ritz, and the company of Mary Welsh.

The Fourth Infantry Division had been pulled off the front for six weeks of rest and retraining. Ernest spent much of this time partying at the Ritz and touring Montmartre bars and nightclubs with Mary and scores of other friends. Marlene Dietrich was entertaining troops at shows sponsored by the United Service Organizations but found time to visit Ernest frequently in the Ritz bar.

In a letter to Max Perkins, Ernest said he planned to write a novel based on his war experiences. It would include submarine patrols, RAF flights, and infantry battles. The book was still in the planning stage, however, when he rejoined the Twenty-second Regiment in mid-November. Lanham and his men were now up against strong defenses west of the German city of Düren. Ernest appeared at regimental headquarters carrying a submachine gun and wearing a white German jacket. He brought a generous supply of whiskey. He and Lanham stayed up late that night drinking and trading war stories.

The next day, Ernest experienced another strange premonition. The regiment was preparing an attack, and after Ernest and Lanham inspected a battalion outpost, Lanham expressed doubts about the ability of the major in charge and feared he might have to relieve him of command. Ernest said the man "stinks of death" and that Lanham need not worry about relieving him.

When the two friends returned to Lanham's command post, they learned that the major had just been killed by a shell fragment. Lanham looked at Ernest with astonishment. Ernest could not explain how he had known.

The attack was costly. German shells, exploding in tree-tops, blasted shrapnel over a wide swath. The ground was heavily mined, and German mortar fire was steady and accurate. Sleet, snow, and cold wind helped slow the advance. Ernest spent his days in the field and his nights at headquarters with Lanham and his officers.

Although he never took unnecessary chances, he was always cool under fire, and with memory of his interrogation about activities not allowed correspondents still fresh, he fired his submachine gun just once. This was when several Germans attacked Lanham's command post, killing one officer. Ernest, one of the first to react, charged with gun blazing. He was joined quickly by others, and the attack was soon repelled.

By now, however, the Twenty-second Regiment was weak and vulnerable. Fortunately, Lanham was wise enough to make up a reserve unit out of signalmen, mechanics, and other members of his headquarters staff. When a German counterattack came, the reserves played a vital role in saving the regiment, but in eighteen days it counted 138 men killed, 184 missing, and 1,859 wounded. On December 4, as the battalion pulled out of action, Ernest headed back to Paris.

He went to bed with a severe cold and heavy worries. Bumby was missing in action. Marty had decided to file for divorce. Ernest had begun making plans to go home when the Germans put all their motorized armor into a massive counter-attack. Although still ill, he hurried north to cover what soon became known as the Battle of the Bulge. He missed much of the action when a relapse forced him back to bed, but again he reconstructed the action for his dispatches from interviews.

Ernest's health had returned when Marty arrived to cover the story. She and Ernest spent most of their time together squabbling.

Back at the Ritz in January, he learned that Bumby was alive. After parachuting behind enemy lines to help organize partisan resistance, he had been wounded in the right arm and shoulder and taken prisoner. He was reportedly recovering well in a German prison camp.

During this period in Paris, many officers on leave from the Twenty-second Regiment enjoyed Ernest's hospitality at the Ritz. Buck Lanham's arrival in February called for a party. Ernest got drunk, put a photo of Noel Monks, Mary's husband, in the toilet, and blasted it with several shots from a pair of German pistols. The shots also shattered the toilet and flooded the bathroom. Ernest thought it was funny, but Mary was so disgusted she almost walked out forever. Later he agreed with her that it was time for him to go home and try to put his life in order.

Ernest's return to civilian life after World War I had been difficult; the adjustment after World War II was a painful ordeal. In New York, he collected Patrick and Gregory, on spring vacation from their boarding schools, and headed for Cuba. He wanted to prepare the Finca for Mary's promised arrival. He wanted to regain his health, and he wanted to start writing again.

Fixing up the Finca kept him busy for several days. He recruited a staff of house servants and four gardeners. When the boys returned to school, he began a regular regime of exercises, but his health worried him. He still had headaches and was troubled by slow speech and loss of memory. His old friend Dr. José Luis Herrera, shocked that Ernest had gone on drinking after his concussion in London, said he must stop drinking until the headaches went away. Ernest cut down but did not stop drinking entirely. Nevertheless, his health gradually returned.

He swam, played tennis, and worked around the estate. He won top money at his gun club in a pigeon-shooting contest. He took *Pilar* to sea, wearing nothing but a jockstrap in order to get a good tan. On April 19 he finished thatching the poolhouse roof, swam ten laps, did seventy-five lifting exercises, sorted books to go into a new bookcase, shot pigeons—scoring hits on nineteen out of twenty birds—played three sets of tennis, and finished up with more swimming. It was a memorable day, but he still could not write. Most evenings he drank and felt lonely and depressed.

This continued until May 2, when Mary Welsh arrived in Cuba. She was delighted with the Finca, and even more pleased with Ernest's improved health. He had lost weight, and he had a deep tan. Mary, who loved to swim and fish, soon proved useful on *Pilar*. When Patrick, Gregory, and Bumby, liberated at last from prison camp, arrived at the Finca, Mary was an instant hit with the boys. She saw to it that the undernourished Bumby received plenty of food and rest. When his health returned, Ernest took him to the Floridita bar and bragged about Bumby's war record.

Then the summer was spoiled by another accident. Mary was scheduled to fly to Chicago on June 20 to see to her divorce from Noel Monks. It was raining when Ernest began driving her to the airport. He hit a slippery spot, and the car skidded, soared over a ditch, and slammed into a tree. Mary suffered a deep cut on her left cheek. Ernest had a bruised head, four broken ribs, and a painfully swollen knee. His first concern, however, was to get Mary to a plastic surgeon to repair her cut.

Both needed several weeks to recuperate. Mary did not fly to Chicago until late August. Ernest's health continued to improve. His headaches were still severe, but they were less frequent. He had not, however, done any serious writing since his return to Cuba.

Mary was still in Chicago when Buck Lanham, now a brigadier general, arrived with his wife, Pete, for a two-week vacation. Although Ernest and Buck got along as well as ever, Buck's wife was too outspoken to suit Ernest. She said bull-fighting was a cruel sport. She usually took Marty's side when he described his recent marital difficulties. And after Ernest described his mother as a shrew who had driven his father to suicide, Pete concluded that Hemingway was a hopeless woman hater. Mary tried to bring a truce when she returned, but the breach between Ernest and Pete remained wide when the Lanhams left.

Ernest tried again to get his war book started. Sale of movie rights for "The Killers" and "The Short Happy Life of Francis Macomber" for a total $112,500 had been encouraging, but 1945 came to an end with little promise of a new beginning.

Ernest's divorce from Marty Gellhorn had become final in December, and three months later, Mary was free to marry. The ceremony took place in the office of a Havana lawyer on March 14, 1946. Conducted mostly in Spanish and entirely under the old civil laws of Cuba, the ritual took most of the day. When the newlyweds returned to the Finca hot and exhausted, Ernest started an argument that almost set Mary packing. Next day, however, peace returned to the house on the hill. And Ernest began writing at last.

It was not the war novel that got him started but a rambling story based on his experiences with previous wives, especially Hadley and Pauline. *The Garden of Eden,* as he called it, was experimental and well below his usual standard. Its central characters were two young couples who seemed to have few interests other than making love. Ernest was not sure how the narrative would end, but he did enjoy writing the love scenes.

In July, when Mary announced that she was expecting a baby, Ernest at once arranged for a Sun Valley vacation. He was eager to introduce Mary to his Idaho friends and show her the resort; but he had trouble getting her there alive.

Chapter 22

Italy Revisited

ON AUGUST 19, MARY LAY DYING IN NATRONA COUNTY
Memorial Hospital. Her pregnancy was tubular. That morning,
an internal rupture had roused her in great pain at a motel in
Casper, Wyoming. Ernest had rushed her to the hospital, but
she had continued to lose strength under the care of a hospital
intern.

Toward the end of the day, as Mary's pulse weakened,
the intern pulled off his gloves and advised Ernest to say good-
bye to his wife. Ernest reacted quickly and decisively. He
donned a surgeon's mask and gown and insisted that the intern
probe for a vein. As soon as the needle was inserted, Ernest
cleared a tube and fed a bottle of blood plasma into Mary's
arm. Her pulse soon strengthened. Her breathing returned to
normal.

Ernest stayed with her until the hospital surgeon, who
had been on a fishing trip, appeared. He put Mary in an oxygen
tent and gave her four more pints of plasma and two pints of
whole blood. A week later, out of danger at last, she told Ernest
he was a good man to have around in times of trouble.

The boys, who had been waiting in Sun Valley, came to

Casper to fish with their father. Early in September, the family settled into Sun Valley at last.

It was the best season for hunting and fishing that Ernest could remember. They dined on game nearly every night. Patrick shot a buck that provided venison for several days. Mary's health improved steadily.

After seeing a private screening of *The Killers,* starring Burt Lancaster and Ava Gardner, Ernest declared that Hollywood at last had made a successful adaptation of his work.

On the drive east, during a stopover in New Orleans, Ernest met Mary's parents for the first and last time. From there, the Hemingways went to New York for a three-week visit. They had pleasant reunions with many friends, but the stay included an embarrassing evening for Mary in the fashionable Stork Club. The Hemingway party was seated not far from a table where Ingrid Bergman was dining with the veteran actor Charles Boyer. Ernest began drunkenly baiting Boyer with insults. The suave Boyer ignored the assault as Mary, Buck Lanham, and other friends tried vainly to quiet Ernest.

Mary was glad to return to Cuba, where Ernest could resume his regular routine. The first months of 1947 found him working on *The Garden of Eden.* Although he knew it was not a best-seller, he continued working at it diligently into April, until Patrick arrived and fell seriously ill.

He and Gregory had been in a traffic accident while visiting Pauline in California. Their injuries were thought minor, but when Patrick arrived complaining of a headache, Ernest immediately suspected a concussion. On April 14, Patrick woke with a fever, was soon delirious, and by evening became violent.

Mary was away visiting her ill father, but Ernest organized the servants into a nursing staff and converted the Finca into a hospital. Patrick, often unconscious, had to be fed rectally.

Ernest watched over him day and night, catching no more than a few minutes of sleep at a time until Pauline appeared to help. She had heard tales of Ernest's public drunkenness and was delighted to find him sober and competent. When Mary returned on May 18, Patrick was making a good recovery, and much to Ernest's amusement, Pauline and Mary liked each other at once.

In June, soon after returning from ceremonies at the United States embassy in Havana, where Ernest received the Bronze Star for his work as a war correspondent, the Hemingways learned that Max Perkins had died unexpectedly. Ernest was devastated. Perkins had been a loyal friend and one of the best editors of the century.

Ernest's own health failed him in August. At 256 pounds, he was seriously overweight. His blood pressure was dangerously high. Dr. Herrera put him on a strict diet. Ernest hoped a Sun Valley vacation would restore his health.

He made the trip to Idaho in September alone. Mary and Pauline stayed at the Finca to see Patrick through the final stages of his convalescence. Mary also stayed behind to supervise the construction of a three-story observation tower she had designed. The tower would include an office for Ernest and a special room for the cats. The top would be a sunbathing deck and give a glorious view of the estate.

Mary and Pauline got on so well together that they agreed to meet again in California with Bumby, Patrick, and Gregory over the Thanksgiving weekend. Meanwhile, Ernest's health improved. He did not like spending Thanksgiving alone in Idaho, but he was pleased to drop twenty-eight pounds and bring his blood pressure down. The snow came early, and when Mary appeared after Thanksgiving, they were able to ski. They stayed into the winter.

When they headed for home on February 1, the Hemingways had a passenger. Blackie, or Black Dog, was a springer spaniel who soon became Ernest's loyal friend.

Later in the month, after settling once again in the Finca, he was interviewed by Malcolm Cowley for a long article in *Life* magazine. Ernest also began corresponding with Lillian Ross, a profile writer for the *New Yorker* magazine. Later, Aaron Edward Hotchner came to Cuba asking Ernest to write about the future of literature for *Cosmopolitan*.

Hotchner, a Hemingway fan since his youth in St. Louis, Missouri, was now in his midtwenties and still in awe of the great man. Ernest treated Hotchner to several drinks at the Floridita bar and next day took him fishing on *Pilar*. It was the start of a close friendship.

With all his interviewers, Ernest added to the Hemingway legend. He urged Cowley, for instance, to get a description of his performance in the war from Lanham, knowing that Buck would praise his courage and military savvy to the skies. In his letters to Miss Ross, he recommended other likely candidates for her profiles, thus putting himself in the role of a selfless friend. Of course, he did not tell interviewers that he had been unable to get his war novel started, or that *The Garden of Eden* was well below his earlier standards.

Meanwhile, when a reporter from *McCall's* magazine sought to interview his mother, Ernest exploded with wrath and ordered her not to grant the interview. He and Grace were no longer on good terms, and he was convinced that her recollections of his youth would destroy the "tough kid" image he wanted to maintain.

Italy had been much on Ernest's mind. Perhaps he thought if he returned he could recapture some of the spirit and enthusiasm that had motivated *A Farewell to Arms*. So instead of going to Sun Valley, he and Mary decided to spend the fall of 1948 in Italy.

Meanwhile, they took long fishing cruises on *Pilar*. On his forty-ninth birthday, Mary gave him a boat party with gifts from many friends, including some of the Finca's cats. Ernest was delighted.

The Hemingways' September arrival in Italy was an event. Ernest was an international celebrity by now, and many Italians remembered that Hemingway had been decorated by their government as a war hero. From the moment their ship docked at Genoa, the Hemingways were warmly received everywhere. His Italian publishers told him that translations of his novels were outselling all other novels published since World War II. Later, in Venice, Ernest received a scroll naming him a cavalier in the Knights of Malta. Once settled into the Gritti Palace Hotel in Venice, Ernest's regular visits to Harry's Bar made the place famous.

From Venice he made a special trip to Fossalta and found the spot where he had been wounded in 1918. He buried a one-thousand-lire note so that he could say he had given both blood and money to Italy. The little ritual inspired him. He returned to Venice eager to write again. He and Mary found a quiet inn on Torcello, an island an hour north of Venice by boat. Through most of November, while Mary traveled through northern Italy with friends, Ernest followed a working routine. He wrote in the mornings and shot ducks in the afternoons.

Early in December Ernest was invited to go partridge shooting on an estate south of Latisana. While there, Ernest met eighteen-year-old Adriana Ivancich of Venice. Her dark hair, hazel eyes, and soft voice appealed to Ernest. He began calling her "daughter," and invited her to lunch to meet Mary. Adriana, flattered by Ernest's attention, had no idea that she would become the model for a character in a Hemingway novel.

Ernest and Mary spent Christmas in Cortina d' Ampezzo, where they cut a fir from the nearby forest for their tree. He

Adriana Ivancich's youth and dark beauty fascinated Ernest. He and Mary saw her often in Venice. (A. E. Hotchner)

planned to devote most of the coming year to his long-delayed war book, but 1949 began badly. Mary broke her ankle skiing and hobbled about in a cast for six weeks. Ernest went to bed with a cold for two weeks. In March, a small scratch on his left eye became infected and the swelling spread across his face. He began running a fever. Cortina doctors sent him to a hospital in Padua for heavy doses of penicillin. Both eyes were swollen shut and his face was crusted with dead skin before the infection began to subside.

Both healthy again at last, Mary and Ernest returned to the Gritti Palace in Venice, where they entertained Adriana Ivancich and her brother, Gianfranco, at lunch. Gianfranco had served under General Erwin Rommel in North Africa, had been wounded, and had returned to Italy. He joined the invading Allies as an OSS officer and was almost shot by Italian criminals at the end of the war. Ernest was fascinated by the story and encouraged the young man to come to Cuba.

While still in Venice, Ernest started a new book. It was not exactly the war novel he had planned, but his hero was a forty-nine-year-old army colonel who, like Ernest, had been wounded on the Italian front in the first war and returned thirty years later at the end of another war with failing health. Ernest was still working on the plot when he and Mary went to Genoa to board their ship for home.

Ernest returned to the Finca in good spirits. He was writing again and, this time, pleased with what he wrote. He drank less, his health improved, his energy increased. He worked diligently for several weeks, not taking a break until June, when it was time to fish in the Bahamas with his boys. Gregory developed an inflamed appendix, and a navy crashboat rushed him to the mainland for an emergency operation, but all ended well.

Ernest celebrated his fiftieth birthday on *Pilar* with five friends and a case of champagne, but he was eager to return to the new book. He thought it might be his best novel. He hoped to finish it before he and Mary returned to Europe again in the fall.

In September, with some forty-five thousand words written, he picked a shortened version of General Stonewall Jackson's dying words for the title. *Across the River and into the Trees* would again echo Ernest's preoccupation with death, but the book would also be a love story. He had Cantwell, his dying hero, fall in love with Renata, a nineteen-year-old Italian countess. She, of course, was modeled on Adriana Ivancich.

There were just a few more pages of the first draft to write when Ernest and Mary flew to New York in mid-November to meet Lillian Ross. She began her interviews for the *New Yorker* profile on Ernest, but a parade of friends in their hotel interrupted her work constantly. She had many questions still to ask when the Hemingways sailed for France.

Chapter 23

The Old Man and the Sea

SOON AFTER THE HEMINGWAYS SETTLED INTO THE Ritz Hotel in Paris, Ernest finished the first draft of the novel and began revisions. Meanwhile, A. E. Hotchner, the young editor from *Cosmopolitan*, arrived to collect early installments of the book for the magazine, which was about to serialize it.

"Hotch," as he was now called, listened avidly to Ernest's stories and was full of praise and admiration. Ernest, gratified by his young friend's attention, was eager to show him around the city. After a morning of work, Ernest spent the afternoon with Hotchner. If it was raining, they took long walks together. If it was fair, they went to the steeplechase races at Auteuil, where they tried to develop a profitable betting system.

Ernest's enthusiasm and confidence were infectious. He was soon placing bets for customers at the Ritz bar and members of the hotel staff. On one memorable day, Hotch and Ernest backed a horse that finished first and paid off on 232 to 10 odds. Ernest stood at the Ritz bar that evening proudly distributing the winnings.

On Christmas Eve, Ernest, Mary, and Hotchner left for the south of France in a large Packard that Ernest had rented.

He sat beside the driver and demonstrated his remarkable memory and historical knowledge with a continous commentary on the passing countryside. At Nice, Hotchner took the train back to Paris while Ernest and Mary prepared to continue their journey to Venice.

January in Italy was a continuous party. Ernest's aristocratic friends were eager to entertain the Hemingways on their estates, and Ernest, with another major work all but finished, was eager to celebrate. He drank heavily.

In Venice, Ernest and Mary discovered a tavern where they could drink and sing most of the evening. They would rise next day in time to entertain guests for luncheon. Adriana Ivancich was a frequent guest, and although Ernest's relationship with her remained platonic, his attentions disturbed Mary.

Early in February, they went to Cortina. Mary skied and Ernest continued his revisions. He developed another skin infection and again had to take heavy doses of penicillin. Then Mary broke her ankle on the slopes where she had suffered a break the year before. She was free of her cast, however, in time to start the journey home.

In Paris, Ernest came down with a cold. He was still ill and depressed when they sailed from Le Havre on March 22, 1951. In New York, Lillian Ross resumed her interviews and the attention revived his spirits. Patrick, now a student at Harvard, came down to see Ernest. He also saw Chink Smith, one of his many other visitors. Chink had read the first installments of *Across the River and into the Trees* in *Cosmopolitan*, and praised Ernest's sensitive treatment of a retired military officer. Ernest, Chink said, had captured the sorrow and the thoughts of the character perfectly. Ernest glowed in the praise.

Back at the Finca in early April, Ernest's dark mood returned. Three letters waiting for him from Adriana failed to cheer him. He knew his love for her was hopeless and he vented his frustration on Mary. One day when he was supposed to meet Mary and her visiting cousin for lunch in Havana he arrived late with one of the city's more famous prostitutes on his arm. Later, he taunted Mary with descriptions of other Havana prostitutes.

He was upset about his inability to write. He sometimes talked dramatically of suicide. On May 13, 1950, Lillian Ross's profile on Hemingway finally appeared in the *New Yorker*. Many readers thought it shattered his image, that it was devastating, but Ernest reacted with apparent indifference.

Meanwhile, Gianfranco Ivancich, Adriana's brother, had taken Ernest's advice and come to Cuba. Ernest found him a job. In June, with his generous mood restored, he and Mary spent five happy days on *Pilar*. When they went cruising again in July, however, Ernest slipped on the wet deck, bruised his back, and cut his beleaguered head. His headaches returned. So did his depression.

Reviews of *Across the River and into the Trees* darkened his mood. Some critics called the book trivial, even embarrassing. Several said the book read like a parody of the earlier Hemingway work. In England, where the reviews were also generally bad, one critic concluded that the book was out of fashion.

Veteran American author John O'Hara was one of the few to praise the book. He said Hemingway was the most important writer since Shakespeare.

As if headaches weren't enough, Ernest began suffering severe pain in his right leg. X rays showed that his fall had shifted 1918 shell fragments, which now pressed against nerves and veins. Swimming in seawater, Ernest found, was good therapy, but it took a long time for the pain to abate. His dark moods continued.

Once, at a dinner party, he embarrassed Mary by putting his plate on the floor, untouched. He often scolded and humiliated her in front of their friends. Mary, however, seemed to have unlimited patience.

Ernest's high spirits and enthusiasm returned with a rush in late October when Adriana and her mother arrived for a long visit. The girl was never out of her mother's sight, but she treated the graying author with flattering kindness and respect. He was in love again.

Under the mother's alert eye, Ernest took Adriana pigeon shooting and fishing on *Pilar*. When they went to Havana nightclubs, Ernest did not dance with Adriana, explaining very seriously that he wanted to avoid scandal.

Mary was delighted by Adriana's beneficial influence. Ernest followed his diet, cut back on his drinking, lost weight, and began writing again. The creative energy seemed limitless. Day after day, he rose early and wrote all morning. He had an ambitious plan. For three weeks he worked on a story he called "The Sea When Absent," which he saw as part of a three-part novel. *The Garden of Eden* would be the second part, and a yet unwritten part called "The Sea in Being" would be the third.

The holidays and a string of visitors, including Patrick and his bride, Henny, and Gregory with a girlfriend, interrupted his work. After the New Year, however, he resumed writing with the same energy as before. This time he worked on "The Sea in Being," using the tale Carlos Gutiérrez had told him years before about the old fisherman who, after a heroic battle with a marlin, loses the fish to sharks. He turned out one thousand words a day, well over his usual quota.

He continued at the same pace even after Adriana and

her mother left in early February. By February 17, the story, totaling some twenty-six thousand words, was all but finished. The old fisherman, whom Ernest called Santiago, had returned to port with nothing but the skeleton of a huge fish to show for his heroic struggle. Ernest was amazed at his own heroic accomplishment. Never had the words flowed so quickly and never had he had as much satisfaction from a major work. The story of the old man's endurance and perseverance obviously found resonance in Hemingway's personality.

While still on the productive schedule, he wrote a story based on his wartime submarine hunting. It ended with the death of the Hemingway-style hero. The words continued to flow, but Ernest knew that the second story was no match for the story of Santiago. Vera and Charles Scribner, Aaron Hotchner, and several other Finca visitors who read it were unstinting in their praise of the story. Ernest decided to call it *The Old Man and the Sea*.

He sent the manuscript to Carlos Baker, a Princeton professor who was preparing a critical appraisal of Hemingway's work and would one day write his biography. Baker said Santiago reminded him of Shakespeare's King Lear.

Ernest's mood mellowed. When news came of his mother's death at age seventy-nine, he forgot his animosity and mourned her. On the day of her funeral, he saw to it that the old bell at the Finca began tolling at dawn. He was more tender with Mary. When she left early in July to visit family and friends, Ernest wrote to her almost daily telling how greatly she was missed.

Mary returned in August, but was called away almost at once to her sick father's bedside. Ernest complained of loneliness and said he was surrounded by sickness and death. Many of his Cuban friends were seriously ill. Then news came of

Pauline's death in California at the age of fifty-six. Ernest was shocked. She had died suddenly on October 2 of an undiagnosed tumor.

Ernest was greatly relieved when Mary returned, but death continued to haunt them into 1952. In January, Mary's maid committed suicide. A few weeks later they received the news that Charles Scribner had died.

For several days Ernest felt abandoned. It seemed there was no one left in the publishing business whom he could trust. A New York publisher restored his faith by saying *The Old Man and the Sea* should be published in full in a single issue of *Life* magazine. The suggestion prompted Ernest to write Wallace Meyer, now his editor at Scribner's, proposing that the story be published as a short novel. Meyer endorsed the idea and reported a few weeks later that the Book of the Month Club wanted to buy the rights. This news was followed by a cable from *Life.* The magazine would pay forty thousand dollars to print the book in a special September 1952 issue, thus putting *The Old Man and the Sea* into the hands of five million readers. No other American novel had been offered such wide exposure.

Ernest had been working on *Islands in the Stream,* intended as the opening of his sea book, but set it aside to prepare *The Old Man and the Sea* for its various publications. This kept him busy through the remaining months of 1952. Meanwhile, when Scribner's offered a cover design he did not like, he wrote Adriana Ivancich, a competent artist, asking her to try something. Her stylized view of a fishing village and harbor delighted Ernest, and he forwarded it to Scribner's.

He had great hopes for the book, but the early reviews went far beyond his expectations. William Faulkner said *The Old Man and the Sea* might prove to be the best book from the current generation of writers. Some others who saw advance copies of the galleys said it might be the best book of the century. Ernest glowed. He was most touched, however, when his Italian translator wrote that she had wept over the book for an entire afternoon.

Ernest decided that it was good, very good indeed.

Chapter 24

Reported Dead

ADVANCE SALES OF THE REGULAR EDITION OF *THE Old Man and the Sea* hit 50,000 and weekly sales averaged 3,000 after publication. Advance sales of the London edition were 20,000, with 2,000 in weekly sales. *Life* sold 5,318,560 copies of its special edition.

Meanwhile, congratulatory telegrams, phone calls, and letters deluged the Finca. The letters alone totaled eighty to ninety a day. It seemed that a Hollywood producer wanted the movie rights. Ministers quoted from the book in their sermons. Reviewers raved.

The art critic Bernard Berenson called the book a masterpiece with a style worthy of Homer. Cuba gave Ernest the Medal of Honor.

The only negative comment came from his son Gregory, who said the book was sentimental slop. At twenty-one, Gigi was fiercely independent and outspoken. He in particular was resentful of Ernest's treatment of Pauline.

Many friends urged Ernest to go to New York to revel in the glory, but he preferred to fish and make plans for another trip to Africa. Patrick and his wife were living on a ranch in

Kenya, and his enthusiastic letters made Ernest yearn for a safari.

Departure had to be delayed, however, in order to negotiate sale of movie rights to *The Old Man and the Sea.* Ernest was annoyed that the business lasted through most of the spring of 1953. He met Spencer Tracy and said the veteran actor would be all right for the part of Santiago. Later Ernest regretted the decision. In April he agreed to a $25,000 advance and another $25,000 to supervise the fishing sequences needed for the film.

Meanwhile, he was annoyed by several authors who wanted to write his biography. He protested repeatedly that he would not authorize a biography while he was still alive.

In May, while Ernest and Mary were on board *Pilar,* news came over the radio that *The Old Man and the Sea* had won a Pulitzer Prize. Ernest, who could not forget that an earlier nomination for *For Whom the Bell Tolls* had been vetoed, referred to the award as the "Pullover Prize." But he was deeply gratified just the same.

In June, Ernest and Mary went to New York and boarded a ship for France. He was eager to spend several weeks in Spain before heading for East Africa. They arrived in Le Havre on June 30 and left immediately for Pamplona by car. The town was full of bullfight fans and tourists. Every hotel room was taken. Ernest and Mary had to go north twenty miles to Lecumberri to find a place to stay.

Early the next day scores of old friends were waiting to greet Papa at Pamplona's main gate. Spaniards, who had not seen him since the civil war, welcomed Ernest as a returning hero. The hero of the season in the bullring was Antonio Ordoñez, the son of Cayetano Ordoñez, whom Ernest had used as the prototype for Pedro Romero, the matador in *The*

After a day's hunt, Ernest and Philip Percival exchange stories and enjoy a drink by the fire. (Look photo by Earl Thiesen)

Sun Also Rises. Ernest introduced himself to the young man and congratulated him for his good work.

Heavy rains spoiled the fiesta soon after it started, and when Mary caught a bad cold, the Hemingways left for Madrid ahead of schedule. Madrid filled him with nostalgia. In the Hotel Florida he found the room he had used as headquarters in 1937. He celebrated his fifty-fourth birthday there among the ghosts.

From Madrid, the Hemingways went to a villa near Saelices to visit Ordoñez and his brother-in-law, Luis Miguel Dominguín, another excellent matador. At Valencia they saw more bullfights before heading north for France. They had only a few nights in the Ritz before it was time to go to Marseilles and board the ship for Mombasa.

They suffered through Egypt's August heat, but the ship was more comfortable than the one that took Pauline and Ernest to Kenya in 1933, and they docked at Mombasa in a refreshing rainstorm. Philip Percival, twenty years older but as cheerful and enthusiastic as ever, took them to a guest camp on his nearby farm. A photographer, Earl Thiesen, arrived to take pictures for *Look* magazine. They would go with the articles that Ernest had agreed to write. At the end of August, they gathered equipment and made final preparations for the safari.

Soon after heading south for the Kajiado District, forty miles from Nairobi, ranger Denis Zaphiro stopped the party. A wounded rhinoceros he had been tracking was standing in the shade of a nearby thornbush. Zaphiro offered Ernest the chance to kill it. Armed with his heaviest rifle, he took his first shot from twelve yards. When the rhino spun around, Ernest fired again. The beast ran. Although the rhino left a trail of blood, night closed in before they could track the animal. Next

Ernest enjoyed his authority as an honorary African game warden. Here he takes the pulse of a sick native. (Look photo by Earl Thiesen)

morning, however, after camping nearby, Ernest and Zaphiro found the rhino dead. So ended Ernest's first kill, and so began a new friendship.

Zaphiro was an expert on African wildlife and his great zeal for conserving it gratified Ernest. Percival, taking note of the new friendship, asked Zaphiro to serve as the party's white hunter. Later, Zaphiro managed to have Ernest appointed honorary game warden in one of the hunting regions.

When Masai villagers complained of marauding lions, Zaphiro and Ernest put out several zebra carcasses for bait and stood watch for the prey. They had a long wait, but Ernest finally got a shot from two hundred yards. He wounded the lion, but he and Zaphiro were able to track it down and kill it easily. It was not Ernest's best shooting, but in camp he boasted about it endlessly.

Like Charles Thompson twenty years earlier, Mayito Menocal, a Cuban sportsman, was collecting better trophies than Ernest. Again Ernest's competitive spirit tormented him. After Menocal killed a huge, black-maned lion with a single shot, Ernest had a series of embarrassing misses. Soon a water buffalo, two lions, two zebras, a warthog, and a baboon all owed their lives to Hemingway's poor marksmanship. Mary had better luck, but had still not shot her lion when the party returned to Nairobi for a rest.

Ernest, with his weight down to 190 pounds, was more fit than he had been in years, and he looked forward eagerly to more hunting. Meanwhile, he left Mary at the Percival farm to fly south to Tanganyika (Tanzania) to visit Patrick and Henny, who had just acquired a three-thousand-acre farm there.

When he returned late in October, Menocal and Thiesen the photographer had both left. Ernest and Mary were eager to go into the wilds alone. Their luck was poor. They found game scarce and the heat almost unbearable in the Usangu District. Temperatures rose to 114 degrees. Then, on a sharp turn in the road, Ernest fell out of the Land Rover and suffered a shoulder sprain and facial cuts.

While convalescing, he developed an interest in Debba, one of the native girls who visited their camp. Although his interest in Debba waned, a few days later, he dyed his jackets and shirts with native ocher and tried hunting with a spear. His native phase ended when he was asked to hunt elephants that had been damaging crops. The request made him take his duties as honorary game warden seriously.

For Christmas, the Hemingways decorated a thorn tree and gave gifts to the native members of the safari. Later, the safari scouts, sporting dyed ostrich plumes, danced for the hunters. New Year's Eve was quieter, marked with tea and mince pies supplied by the Percivals. Mary and Ernest congratulated themselves on their good fortune.

Fortune, however, was about to take a bad turn.

As a belated Christmas present for Mary, Ernest had hired a bush pilot to fly them in his Cessna 180 over some of the most scenic parts of Africa, including the famous Murchison (now Kabalega) Falls in Uganda. The flight began on January 21, 1954. All went well until they reached the falls and the pilot began circling to give Mary a chance to take pictures. On his final pass, the pilot had to dive to avoid a flight of ibis. The plane struck a telegraph wire stretched across the gorge. The wire damaged the propeller and the tail assembly, and the plane began to lose altitude. The pilot managed to pancake onto a level patch of thornbushes three miles southwest of the falls. The plane was wrecked, but there was no fire and apparently no serious injuries. Mary, however, was in shock, with a weak pulse and a painful chest. Ernest, who had a sprained right shoulder, made her lie down until her pulse returned to normal. The pilot tried vainly to call for help over the plane's radio. When night fell, the three huddled by an open fire, sleeping only fitfully.

*Africa delighted Mary and Ernest during most of their visit in 1953–1954. Here Mount Kilimanjaro provides the background. (*Look* photo by Earl Thiesen)*

At first light, while gathering wood, Ernest was surprised to see a tour boat on the river. After much waving and shouting, he got the crew's attention, and when the boat stopped at a dock below, a party of natives began climbing toward the wrecked plane.

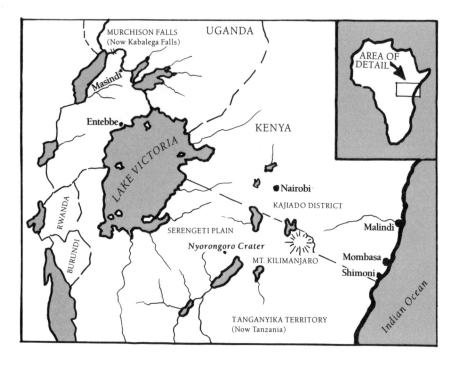

It turned out that the boat had been hired out of Lake Albert by a British doctor and his family. They had left the boat to walk to the base of the falls, but when they returned, they agreed to take the Hemingways back to the Lake Albert port of Butiaba. The return to civilization was like a return from the grave.

Earlier in the day, a commercial pilot had spotted the wrecked Cessna with no sign of life and the news had flashed around the world that the Hemingways were missing and presumed dead. Many papers had printed Ernest's obituary. Famous contemporaries had lamented his loss and praised his talent. Ernest, however, was alive and eager to bring the ill-fated venture to an end.

Another bush pilot offered to fly the Hemingways to Entebbe on the north shore of Lake Victoria, where they could catch a commercial flight to Nairobi.

The survivors were near exhaustion when they arrived at Butiaba airport. Their twelve-passenger De Havilland looked safe enough, but the airfield looked as if it had just been plowed. They all climbed aboard, however, and were soon jolting and lurching across the primitive field. Suddenly, before it got off the ground, the plane stopped and burst into flame.

Mary quickly unbuckled her seat belt. Her door was jammed, but she crawled to safety through a window. Meanwhile, Ernest butted his way through the jammed door and crawled onto the wing. He jumped to the ground and staggered clear, with blood streaming from his head. Mary, with an injured knee, limped to his aid. Both needed medical attention urgently.

Night had fallen when a policeman drove them over fifty miles of rough road to Masindi. After an uncomfortable night in a rustic hotel, and a visit from a doctor who bandaged Ernest's head, the Hemingways rode one hundred more rough miles by car to reach Entebbe. There they collapsed in the comfort of the Lake Victoria Hotel.

Ernest's head felt like a balloon. He had double vision and sporadic deafness. His face and arms were blistered with first-degree burns. His liver, kidney, and spleen had all been bruised. He had a crushed vertebra and a sprained right arm and shoulder.

Reporters, however, would not leave him alone. They said his survival was a miracle. Ernest agreed.

"My luck," Ernest told them, "she is still good."

The trouble was, he did not feel so good.

Chapter 25

Paris Memoirs

SOON AFTER ERNEST ARRIVED IN NAIROBI BY PLANE, he had a full medical examination. Doctors could not understand what was keeping him alive, and they were amazed at a sudden surge of high spirits and energy.

He sat in bed chuckling over his premature obituaries and savoring scores of letters and telegrams congratulating him on his survival. His escape had stimulated his creative energy, but when he told reporters that he had never been in better health, he was stretching the truth. Just the same, he was able to dictate a fifteen-thousand-word article on the plane crashes for *Look* magazine and answer many of the letters and telegrams. Meanwhile, he and Mary decided to go ahead with plans to charter a boat and set up a fishing camp at Shimoni on the Kenya coast. It was a mistake.

Mary, Patrick and Henny, and the Percivals had already arrived when Ernest flew to the fish camp in mid-February. His back was too painful to attempt fishing, so he stayed in camp while the others went out in the boat. On some days he could barely move, but at times he acted rashly. When a brushfire threatened camp, he tried to help the natives put it out.

He fell into the flames and suffered second-degree burns on his chest, stomach, and legs. The experience seemed to drain what had been left of his energy and enthusiasm.

On the boat from Mombasa to Venice, Ernest rarely left his cabin. He was still a very sick man when he and Mary reached Venice. He took to bed in the Gritti Palace Hotel, feeling weak and depressed. Although he put up a cheerful front for visitors and talked hopefully of visiting Spain, he was too sick to travel for several days.

In April, while Ernest remained in Venice, Mary went on to Paris and London to visit friends. She would meet Ernest in Spain later. Meanwhile, Aaron Hotchner arrived to accompany Ernest to Spain by car. The two companions left Venice in high spirits. Even though Ernest felt nauseated with pain each time he moved, he entertained Hotchner with elaborate stories of past adventures that were often partly true.

When he arrived in Spain, however, he had no enthusiasm for the bullfights. Still tortured by pain, Ernest saw a doctor in Madrid who advised continued rest, a limited diet, and a reduction of alcoholic intake. Ernest followed the regime as he and Mary took a leisurely cruise back to Havana. The sea air helped, and as Ernest read and dozed, some of his strength returned.

His slow recovery continued at the Finca. He swam daily, and he found that a board under his mattress made it easier for him to get to sleep. He could not write. This depressed him and he was impatient with the slowness of his recovery. In the fall of 1954, however, he began a series of stories based on the recent experiences in Africa. One of them, a fictional journal with Mary, Zaphiro, and himself as the main characters, kept expanding until Ernest began to think of it as a novel.

He was well into the project when the wonderful news

came from Sweden that he had won the Nobel Prize for literature with a cash award of thirty-five thousand dollars.

The public announcement on October 28 started a flood of cables, phone calls, and letters. When scores of happy friends appeared at the Finca, Ernest and Mary held a grand party. Ernest was exuberant. He was too ill to accept the award in person, but he recorded a statement to be played when John Cabot, the American ambassador to Sweden, accepted the prize on Hemingway's behalf. Later, Ernest ungraciously complained that the award had distracted him from his writing.

There were more serious distractions soon after 1955 began. In February, Mary's father died after a long illness, and she had to leave Ernest alone for several days. He was lonely and full of self-pity until her return.

They took a trip on *Pilar,* but his sore back and lack of energy made it impossible to enjoy fishing.

Although still far from well, Ernest forgot most of his troubles in early June when movie people arrived to plan filming of *The Old Man and the Sea.* Serving as guide for the visitors and discussing scenes for the picture were stimulating, and after the vistors left, Ernest was delighted to discover that his health had improved.

Friends who came to Cuba at this time, however, were shocked to see how much Ernest had aged. He had the white hair, white beard, and wrinkled face of a man much older than his fifty-six years. Ernest wrote regularly but without his former confidence.

In August, he had to put his long African story aside to prepare for two camera crews that were coming to shoot fishing sequences for *The Old Man and the Sea.* He rented some old boats like the ones native fishermen use, and a cabin cruiser. One camera crew would use *Pilar,* the other the rented cruiser.

Work began in poor weather. Although they landed two marlin the first day, rough seas made filming difficult.

Ernest enjoyed organizing the operation and playing the host with generous supplies of food, drink, and bait, but the bad weather continued and the camera crews went back to Hollywood with disappointing footage.

In mid-November, Ernest suffered a relapse. After receiving Cuba's Order of San Cristóbol in a long ceremony in Havana, he returned to the Finca with a bad cold. This was followed by a kidney infection. His right foot became painfully swollen. His red blood cell count fell dangerously low. Mary, meanwhile, suffered from persistent anemia. Clearly, the Hemingways were still haunted by the African disaster.

Ernest remained in bed until January 9, 1956. He worried about the movie. When Spencer Tracy came to Cuba with a camera crew to begin work on the major scenes for *The Old Man and the Sea*, Ernest said the actor looked too fat and rich to be a convincing Santiago. He was further upset when the producers decided to send a crew to Peru, where the marlin were said to be bigger than those in Cuban waters. Ernest agreed, however, to go Peru to supervise the work.

Rough seas off Lima again made filming difficult. They did not begin to catch anything until after their second week of fishing, but Ernest managed to land a 680-pound marlin without further strain to his back, and when the Hemingways returned to the Finca late in May, both were in improved health.

To his dismay, however, Ernest found he had lost his enthusiasm for the African story. With some reluctance, he accepted an assignment from *Look* magazine for three thousand words to go with the layout of photos that Earl Thiesen had brought back from Africa. *Look* paid five thousand dollars for a job that Ernest rushed out in a day and a half. After that, he worked on rambling stories loosely based on his World War II infantry experiences. They were not good and he knew it.

During an interview soon after his fifty-seventh birthday, Ernest was in such a black mood that he attacked other writers. He called Faulkner a "no-good son of a bitch." Later, in a fit of remorse, he vowed to avoid interviews and public attention.

Hoping another trip to Europe would put him back on track, Ernest booked passage for France in late August. He and Mary first spent two quiet weeks in New York, staying in a friend's home well out of the public eye. In Paris, they stopped briefly at the Ritz before heading south in a rented car. The September weather in Spain was mild. They followed the bull-fights with enthusiasm and cheered Antonio Ordoñez, who was enjoying another heroic season. In Zaragoza, after Aaron Hotchner joined the Hemingways, two bulls were dedicated to Ernest and the crowd gave him a standing ovation. Hotchner, however, was distressed to see that his hero was in poor health and drinking far too much. Hotchner mentioned his concern to Mary. She said she was not going to nag her husband.

Ernest was soon forced to see a doctor again. His blood pressure and cholesterol count were both dangerously high. Ernest's liver was in poor shape, and there was an inflammation around his aorta. The doctor ordered rest and severe limitation of fats and alcohol. Ernest, meanwhile, sometimes lost touch with reality. Despite terrible health, he talked enthusiastically of taking Ordoñez on an African safari.

To Mary's relief, he dropped the scheme, and on November 17 the Hemingways headed back to Paris. They would remain at the Ritz the rest of the year.

During the move into their suite, Ritz porters told Ernest there were two small trunks in storage that bore his name. He had them brought up. The trunks were moldy and covered with dust, but when Ernest opened them he was amazed to find yellow newspaper clips, books, typed and longhand manuscripts, and even some old clothing dating back to his expatriate years in Paris. The trunks were like windows into the past. He carefully repacked everything into two new trunks for the journey home, not fully aware that the seeds had been planted for another book.

The Cuban spring of 1957 was unusually wet and cheerless. Black Dog had died while Ernest was away. Although a new dog had joined the family, Ernest missed his old friend. He worried about Cuban politics. The Batista regime had become oppressive. Many of his friends were afraid. The fishing was poor. He could improve his health with a strict diet, but the regime depressed him, and he was unable to write.

When the *Atlantic Monthly* asked him for an article for its centennial edition, Ernest wrote candidly about his early friendship with F. Scott Fitzgerald. Writing about Scott, however, gave Ernest a growing sense of betrayal. He put the article aside, but several months later, after looking through the old trunks, he got the Fitzgerald piece out again. Why not write sketches of other friends from his early days in Paris? It could be a kind of memoir.

The happy days when Ernest and Hadley were young and full of enthusiasm seemed very remote, but Ernest's memory of that time, prompted by the collection in the trunks, was still good. The collection of sketches gradually grew into a book. Ernest wrote about Gertrude Stein, Ezra Pound, Ford Madox Ford, Sylvia Beach, and many others. Although he showed little kindness to Ford, he wrote about most of his friends with affection. He was pleased that he had managed to write another book. The chronology and organization of the book troubled him. Although he kept changing the sequences of the sketches, he was never fully satisfied. He revised it again and again. He also revised *The Garden of Eden,* a book he had not touched for ten years. He added some new episodes but could not remove the tedious repetitions. He was still struggling with the project in September when he and Mary left Cuba for Sun Valley.

They rented a house in Ketchum, and as soon as they moved in, old friends came by the dozens to welcome them. Again, many were shocked to see how much Ernest had aged, but his spirits and energy revived in the mountain air. He soon began working at his revisions in the mornings and hunting in the afternoons.

He was still following this routine when Fidel Castro overthrew the Batista regime in Cuba. Although he had great hope for the new government, Ernest was not eager to return to Cuba. He spoke of spending the rest of his life in the Rockies.

Chapter 26

Final Days

IN MARCH OF 1959, ERNEST AND MARY PURCHASED A chalet-style house on a seventeen-acre site a mile northwest of downtown Ketchum. It had a large downstairs living room and an equally large upstairs bedroom. A small bedroom at the back could be converted to an office for Ernest. The views were spectacular, and the price was fifty thousand dollars.

They did not take immediate possession. Ernest wanted to spend another season in Spain. He arranged to stay with an old friend who owned a villa near Málaga. It would be a good place to write, and at the same time, it would not be too far from the bullfight centers. Antonio Ordoñez and his brother-in-law Luis Miguel Dominguín were to spend much of the season competing against each other in the ring. Ernest wanted to see each one of the confrontations. By early May, the Hemingways were comfortably established in a large, white house surrounded by a well-tended garden.

Ernest had contracted to do a ten-thousand-word bullfight article for *Life* magazine and had agreed to write a preface for a collection of his short stories to be published for young adults. He went to work at once on the preface, but on May 13 he put it aside to go to Madrid for some of the first bullfights of the season. Ernest's snow white hair and beard were recognized wherever they went.

They followed a vigorous schedule. The fights moved from one city to the next almost daily. Ernest seemed tireless, but Mary soon grew weary. When she caught a cold, she returned to the villa for a welcome rest.

On May 30, when Ordoñez was gored in the left buttock, Ernest insisted on staying with the matador for the first fifty hours of his recovery. A week later, he brought Ordoñez to the villa to supervise his convalescence. Meanwhile, he resumed work on the preface for the collection of stories.

With Ordoñez in the villa, however, Ernest found it difficult to concentrate. He spoke of the young matador as his best friend and became convinced that when Ordoñez faced the bulls again at the end of June he would need the Hemingway luck. Thus it became imperative for Ernest to attend every fight.

It was a difficult summer for Mary. When Ordoñez returned to the ring, Ernest left to resume his hectic schedule. She stayed at the villa, often feeling lonely and neglected. Ernest again overate and drank too much. Mary worried about his health, and she had her own problems.

Early in July, Mary joined Ernest for the week-long festival at Pamplona. She broke her toe while picnicking on the Irati River north of town and had to hobble with a cane for several weeks. Ernest was not sympathetic, and even accused her of faking the injury. Meanwhile, he adopted Valerie Danby-Smith, nineteen, an American journalist, as his personal secretary. Mary, who had already seen Ernest trying to recapture his youth with Adriana, was more amused than worried.

Back at the villa, she staged a lavish party for Ernest's

sixtieth birthday. She hired an orchestra and flamenco dancers, arranged for fireworks, and even set up a small shooting gallery in the garden. She asked many friends and the party lasted through the night. Buck Lanham gave Ernest a copy of the recently finished history of his infantry division. Buck's inscription on the flyleaf moved Ernest so much that he had to retire in tears. Lanham thought that the behavior was out of character. He was also disturbed by Ernest's short temper and his abuse of Mary.

Although he seemed to enjoy himself, Ernest's conversation during the party was full of obscenities. He accused Mary of spending all his money on the party and again made fun of her limp.

Soon after his birthday, Ernest saw Dominguín gored at Valencia. Three days later he saw Ordóñez gored at Palma de Majorca. Although both men were back in action by mid-August, Ernest had become so emotionally involved that every bullfight exhausted him. Meanwhile, he built mountains of notes for his *Life* article. At the end of August, however, after a bull put Dominguín out of action for the rest of the season and Ordóñez suffered a serious foot injury, Ernest had seen enough. He returned to the villa exhausted.

Mary wanted to go home, but Ernest insisted that they stay until he wrote his bullfight article. After he completed five thousand words, however, he realized it was just a beginning and he had much more to write; in mid-October he agreed to continue it at home.

In Paris, he caught a cold that stuck with him all across the Atlantic. In New York, although he had not yet thought of a title, Ernest delivered the Paris memoirs to Scribner's before heading for Cuba. He and Mary entertained Antonio Ordóñez and his wife, Carmen, at the Finca, but Ernest was so eager to show the couple the new house in Ketchum that they stayed in Cuba just a few days.

The drive west gave Ernest the chance to show off the country to his Spanish guests. It was a grand trip, but upon reaching Ketchum, Antonio received an emergency message from a sister in Mexico. She was involved in a domestic crisis and needed his help at once. Carmen and Antonio departed, leaving the Hemingways to move into their new home alone.

On November 27, while hunting birds with Ernest, Mary fell and shattered her left elbow. It took two hours of surgery to reconstruct the shattered joint, and Mary remained in a great deal of pain. Ernest, who was forced to do the household duties, grumbled endlessly. Mary's injury, he said, had ruined the hunting season for both of them. And how could he write when he had to spend all his time running errands?

He wanted to revise the Paris memoirs, and the bullfighting article was still unfinished.

When they returned to the Finca in mid-January 1960, Mary was still in pain and Ernest was still grumbling. The Cuban weather was unusually cold, but Ernest managed to write, and when Valerie Danby-Smith came down to serve as his secretary, he worked with renewed energy. By the end of May, with the bullfight "article" totaling 120,000 words, Ernest declared it finished. He called it *The Dangerous Summer*.

Mentally weary and with eyes tired, he asked Hotchner to come to Cuba to help with revisions. *Life* agreed to pay $90,000 for the rights to print excerpts from the book and $100,000 more for a Spanish translation. First, however, Ernest wanted to cut it back to seventy thousand words. As he and Hotchner struggled with this job, Ernest convinced himself that he must return to Spain for fresh material. He also said Ordoñez needed his luck.

Mary and Hotchner argued against the trip, and although she accompanied Ernest to New York, Mary refused to go to Spain with him. In July, soon after quietly observing his sixty-first birthday, a stubborn Ernest flew alone to Madrid. His memory was failing. He also was suspicious of everyone, and was so troubled with remorse and fear that he could not sleep.

Ernest brought little luck to Ordoñez. In early August, Antonio suffered a concussion, and Carmen had a miscarriage. Ernest asked Valerie to come and help him with his correspondence. She arrived to find him too depressed to do much work. He complained of everything, including his beloved Spain and its bullfights.

He seemed unable to make the decision to go home. In October, he finally agreed to go to Madrid, where Hotchner met him and tried to put him on a flight home. Ernest refused to leave his hotel. He stayed in bed four days, complaining of kidney trouble. Finally, however, he took a midnight flight to New York. There Mary persuaded Ernest to go to Idaho by train. By now he had difficulty talking. It was a struggle for him to complete a sentence.

Mary hoped old friends in Ketchum would cheer Ernest up, but he seemed afraid of everyone. He said the sheriff and FBI agents were after him. His face was pallid. His arms and legs were thin. He walked cautiously, like a very old man.

Dr. George Saviers, Ernest's local doctor, agreed with Mary that Ernest must be hospitalized and have a full physical and psychological examination. Mary, however, did not want Ernest's condition publicly known. On November 30, he was flown secretly in a private plane to the Mayo Clinic in Rochester, Minnesota, where he was registered as "Mr. Saviers."

Doctors were puzzled. Ernest's enlarged liver and mild symptoms of diabetes could both be due to heavy drinking,

Ernest, with a lifelong interest in wildlife, examines an owl found during a hunt near Sun Valley. (A. E. Hotchner)

but the cause for his high blood pressure and severe depression remained a mystery. Doctors prescribed a series of electric shocks, two a week for several weeks, to counter the mental depression. The treatments seemed to help.

On January 11, six weeks after his arrival, Mary let reporters know that Ernest was at the clinic. The news brought stacks of letters. Ernest dictated many replies to a secretary, and the activity cheered him. When doctors released him on

January 22, he seemed to be on the mend and looked forward to returning to Ketchum. He had more revisions in mind for the Paris book. He was still trying to decide what to call it. (It would be published posthumously as *A Moveable Feast*.)

Back at Ketchum again, though he remained at his desk every day from 8:30 A.M. to 1:00 P.M., he accomplished little. He did take good care of himself. He napped and later went walking in the afternoons. He limited his drinking to a little wine with meals. Dr. Saviers came daily to take his blood pressure. There were few other visitors.

Ernest's depression returned one day when, with tears flowing, he told Dr. Saviers that the words wouldn't come anymore. He could no longer write. The painful confession marked the beginning of another decline.

Through March and into April he grew worse and worse. Early one morning, Mary came downstairs to find him at the gun rack holding a double-barreled shotgun and two shells. He had written a note, but when he saw Mary he put it in the pocket of his robe. She never saw it again. She tried vainly to coax Ernest back upstairs, but he did not move or release the gun until Dr. Saviers arrived and took it from him.

The doctor put Ernest under sedation and arranged for his return to the Mayo Clinic. The flight was made on a clear April day over spectacular scenery. Ernest did not seem to notice the view. During much of the flight, he complained that his belt no longer fit him. He was not satisfied until he was loaned a shorter belt that fit him more snugly.

The clinic doctors prescribed another series of shock treatments. Mary, who had been advised to stay home, had lost faith in the treatments. She locked all the guns in a basement storage room and waited.

When Mary finally went to see Ernest in early June, she

Near the end, during a pensive moment in Ketchum, the toll of injuries and illness shows clearly in Ernest's face. (A. E. Hotchner)

thought he looked worse than ever. His doctors, however, insisted that Ernest could be discharged. Mary managed to delay the release until June 26, but then she was forced to drive home with a man she knew to be very sick.

They arrived in Ketchum on Friday, June 30. The trip seemed to have revived him. On July 1 he saw Dr. Saviers and a few other friends, and that night he and Mary dined in a restaurant. Mary began to have hope, but early next morning while she slept, Ernest went downstairs and found the keys to the storeroom. He returned from the basement with the double-barreled shotgun.

In the entrance hallway, he loaded both barrels, placed

the butt of the gun on the linoleum floor, centered his forehead on the twin muzzles, and tripped both triggers. Death came instantly to Ernest Hemingway. It was a bright Sunday morning, July 2, just nineteen days short of his sixty-second birthday.

Epilogue

AFTER ERNEST'S DEATH, MARY HEMINGWAY, JACK "Bumby" Hemingway, Gregory Hemingway, Madelaine "Sunny" Hemingway, Marcelline Hemingway, Leicester Hemingway, Adriana Ivancich, Lloyd Arnold, and A. E. Hotchner all wrote personal memoirs of the man. Mary died in 1986 and is buried beside Ernest under a simple marker in the Ketchum cemetery. Others came to more tragic ends. After severe illnesses sister Ursula and brother Leicester Hemingway both killed themselves, and Adriana Ivancich, who married and had two sons, hanged herself in 1983.

Happily, Jack Hemingway's glamorous daughters, Mariel and Margaux, have brought the Hemingway name more positive attention as actresses and models.

Ernest Hemingway's own work, of course, will remain his most treasured legacy. His short stories and books are still widely read, and dramatizations of his work continue to appear on television and in the movies. The Hemingway "tough guy" hero is still with us. The Hemingway legend survives.

Select
Bibliography

Baker, Carlos. *Ernest Hemingway: A Life Story*. New York: Scribner's, 1969.
————. *Hemingway, the Writer as Artist*. Princeton, N.J.: Princeton University Press, 1972.
Buckley, Peter. *Ernest*. New York: Dial Press, 1978.
Burgess, Anthony. *Ernest Hemingway and His World*. New York: Scribner's, 1978.
Donaldson, Scott. *By Force of Will: The Life and Art of Ernest Hemingway*. New York: Viking Press, 1977.
Hemingway, Gregory H. *Papa: A Personal Memoir*. New York: Paragon House, 1988.
Hemingway, Jack [Bumby]. *Misadventures of a Fly Fisherman: My Life with and without Papa*. New York: McGraw-Hill, 1987.
Hemingway, Mary. *How It Was*. New York: Alfred A. Knopf, 1976.
Hotchner, A. E. *Papa Hemingway*. New York: Random House, 1966.
Kert, Bernice. *The Hemingway Women, Those Who Loved Him—The Wives and Others*. New York: W. W. Norton, 1983.
Lynn, Kenneth S. *Hemingway*. New York: Simon and Schuster, 1987.
Miller, Madelaine Hemingway. *Ernie, Hemingway's Sister "Sunny" Remembers*. New York: Crown Publishers, 1975.
Myers, Jeffrey. *Hemingway: A Biography*. New York: Harper and Row, 1985.
Poore, Charles, ed. *The Hemingway Reader*. New York: Scribner's, 1953.

Books by Ernest Hemingway

Three Stories and Ten Poems, 1923.
in our time, 1923.
In Our Time, 1925.
The Torrents of Spring, 1926.
The Sun Also Rises, 1926.
Men without Women, 1927.
A Farewell to Arms, 1929.
Death in the Afternoon, 1932.
Winner Take Nothing, 1933.
Green Hills of Africa, 1935.
To Have and Have Not, 1937.
The Fifth Column and the First Forty-nine Stories, 1938.
For Whom the Bell Tolls, 1940.
Across the River and into the Trees, 1950.
The Old Man and the Sea, 1952.
The Snows of Kilimanjaro and Other Stories, 1961.

Published Posthumously

A Moveable Feast, 1964.
By-Line: Ernest Hemingway, 1967.
Islands in the Stream, 1970.
The Nick Adams Stories, 1972.
Ernest Hemingway: Selected Letters, 1981.
The Dangerous Summer, 1985.
Dateline: Toronto, 1985.
The Garden of Eden, 1986.
The Complete Short Stories of Ernest Hemingway, 1987.

Index

A

Across the River and into the Trees, 169, 172, 173
Adrianople, 47, 50
African safaris, 87, 92, 99, 100–103, 178– 179, 181–187, 189
"After the Storm," 93
Allington, Floyd, 87
"Along with Youth: A Novel," 61, 76
American Field Service, 21
Anderson, Margaret, 136
Anderson, Sherwood, 40, 42, 44, 64, 65, 69, 96
Anglo-American Press Club, 44
Arnolds, Lloyd, 130, 131, 204
Arnolds, Tillie, 130, 131
Atlantic Monthly, 71, 193
Austria, 58, 59, 67
Autobiography of Alice B. Toklas, The, 96

B

Babbitt, 88
Baker, Carlos, 175
Balmer, Edwin, 35, 37
Battle of the Bulge, 159
Beach, Sylvia, 42, 44, 56–57, 103, 153, 193
Belgium, 153, 154
Benchley, Robert, 67

Berenson, Bernard, 178
Bergman, Ingrid, 136, 164
Best Short Stories of 1926, The, 70
"Big Two-Hearted River," 35, 56, 58
Bimini, 109, 112, 113, 120
Bird, Bill, 44, 48
Bird, Sally, 57
Bone, John, 37, 44, 45, 46, 47, 48, 50, 53
Book of the Month Club, 134, 135, 176
boxing, 15, 36, 37, 40, 42, 43, 48, 57, 68, 70, 71, 109, 112, 127
Boyer, Charles, 164
Briggs, Ellis O., 139
Bronze Star medal, 165
Brooklyn Daily Eagle, 44
Brumback, Ted, 21, 22, 23, 27
"Bull in the Afternoon," 97, 121
Bump, Marjorie, 36
Burton, Harry Payne, 111
Butler, Nicholas Murray, 138

C

"Canary for One, A," 70
Cannell, Kitty, 55, 58, 60
Castro, Fidel, 194
Cézanne, Paul, 43
Charles Scribner's Sons, 65, 71, 73, 110, 123, 134, 135, 176, 197

Chiang Kai-shek, 136, 137
Chicago Daily News, 99
China, 11, 135, 138
Civilian Conservation Corps, 110
Clark, Greg, 37, 53, 145
Collier's magazine, 131, 135, 143, 144, 149
Connable, Harriet, 36
Connable, Ralph, 36
Consolidated Press, 44, 50
Constantinople, 46–47
Cooper, Gary, 95, 134, 136
Cortina d'Ampezzo, 49, 50, 167, 168, 172
Cosmopolitan, 48, 99, 101, 111, 128, 166, 172
Cranston, J. H., 37, 42
"Crook Factory," 141, 142, 143
Cuba, 128–129, 131, 133, 135, 138, 141, 143–144, 159, 161, 169, 173, 178, 190–191, 194, 197–198
  fishing, 93–94, 96–97, 104, 106–107, 113

D

Daily Mail newspaper, 145
Danby-Smith, Valerie, 196, 198, 199
"Dangerous Summer, The," 198
Dark Laughter, 64
Death in the Afternoon, 92, 94, 95, 96, 97
Dietrich, Marlene, 103, 157
Dilworth, Wesley, 5, 6, 16, 19, 35, 36
Domínguín, Luis Miguel, 181, 195, 197
Donne, John, 132
Dorman-Smith, Eric "Chink," 31, 44, 45, 46, 57, 172
Dos Passos, John, 25, 46, 57, 65, 67, 76, 78, 82, 83, 86, 87, 97, 104, 106, 107, 114, 119, 120
Dry Tortugas, 78, 82, 83, 90, 93
Durán, Colonel Gustavo, 120, 143

E

East Africa, 87, 179
Eastman, Max, 97, 121, 122
Ecclesiastes, 64
Egypt, 181
Eleventh International Brigade, 120

England, 61, 144–148, 173, 178, 189
Esquire, 95, 103, 106, 109, 113

F

Farewell to Arms, A, 79, 80, 81, 88, 90, 95, 134, 136, 166
fascism, 45, 72, 116, 132
Faulkner, William, 176, 192
Festival of San Fermin, 51
Fifth Column, The, 123, 127, 128
Fifth Column and the First Forty-nine Stories, The, 127
Fifth Infantry Division, 151
"Fifty Grand," 71
Finca Vigia, 129
Finland, 131
fishing, 21, 35, 38, 57, 62, 73, 79, 80, 82, 83, 84, 86, 93, 95–97, 102–103, 104, 113, 129, 131, 133, 164, 169, 178, 179, 190, 191, 193
Fitzgerald, F. Scott, 61, 65, 69, 113, 121, 135, 193
Fitzgerald, Zelda, 61, 69
Ford, Ford Maddox, 54, 57, 193
Fortune magazine, 82, 145
For Whom the Bell Tolls, 132, 133, 134, 136, 138, 179
"Four Ninety-five Column Marked Down from Five, The," 128
Fourth Infantry Division, 148, 149, 157
France, 84, 121
  Bordeaux, 21–22
  Paris, 40, 42–45, 46, 49, 50, 54–56, 57, 60, 61, 64–65, 67–69, 71–73, 80, 81, 82, 91, 94–95, 98–99, 103, 116, 124, 127–128, 135–136, 145–147, 151–154, 152–153, 157–159, 170–172, 179, 181, 189, 192–193, 197, 198
  postwar visit to, 170–172
Franco, Francisco, 116, 117, 124, 125
Franklin, Sidney, 95, 99, 114, 116, 117

G

Garden of Eden, The, 162, 164, 166, 174, 193
Gardner, John, 96

Gellhorn, Martha. *See* Hemingway, Martha Gellhorn (wife)
Genoa, Italy, 44
Germany, 46, 50, 115, 116, 124, 142, 144, 147–154, 155, 158–159
Gingrich, Arnold, 95, 103, 112
Great Gatsby, The, 61
Greece, 47, 48
Green Hills of Africa, 106, 109, 110
Gritti Palace Hotel, 167, 168, 189
Guthrie, Pat, 62, 63
Gutiérrez, Carlos, 96, 97, 105, 112, 128, 174

H

Hall, Ernest (grandfather), 3, 4, 5, 6
Hayes, Helen, 95
Hemingway, Adelaide (grandmother), 4
Hemingway, Anson (grandfather), 4
Hemingway, Carol (sister), 11, 90, 96
Hemingway, Dr. Clarence Edmonds (father), 3, 4, 6, 7, 8, 12, 14, 16, 19, 20, 21, 27, 34, 35, 38, 41, 71, 77, 80
Hemingway, Ernest
    accidents, 8, 46, 73, 75–76, 83–85, 87, 107, 111, 127, 130, 145, 160, 164, 168, 172–173, 183–184, 187, 189, 198
    African safari, first, 92, 99, 100–103
    African safari, second, 178–179, 181–187, 189
    ambulance service, 21–25
    anti-Semitic attitudes, 13, 58
    battlefield experiences, 22–26
    birth, 3
    Bronze Star award, 165
    childhood, 3, 4, 5, 6, 7, 8–9
    Crook Factory and Q-boat cruising, 141, 142, 143
    D-Day crossing, 146, 147
    death of, 202–203
    early prose and verse, 34, 35, 36, 37, 42, 43, 44, 47–48, 49, 50, 51
    education, 5, 6, 8, 12, 13, 14, 15, 16, 17, 19, 33
    Far East, tour of, 135–138
    fascism, opinions on, 45, 72, 116, 132
    father, relationship with, 7, 8, 11, 12, 13, 14, 16, 20, 21, 34, 35, 38, 71, 77, 80, 161
    foreign correspondent work, 47, 50, 152–159
    France, postwar visit, 170–172
    Genoa, Italy, 44
    hurricane disaster, 109–110
    interrogation at Nancy, 156–157
    journalism of, 16, 19, 20, 21, 27, 38, 47, 50, 152–159
    Kurowsky, Agnes von, love affair, 27–31, 34, 76, 81
    Lausanne, Switzerland, 48
    London, wartime, 144–147
    manuscripts, loss of, 48–49
    mental breakdown, 199–202
    Michigan, first postwar summer, 34–36
    mother, relationship with, 5, 13, 16, 34, 38, 40, 71, 131, 161, 166, 175
    Nobel Prize, 190
    Normandy adventures, 148–153
    Pamplona fiestas, 51, 57, 61, 62, 63
    plane crash, 184–187
    Pulitzer Prize, 179
    recuperation from war wound, 27–35, 40
    Red Cross service, 21–31
    Spanish civil war, involvement in, 113, 114, 116, 117, 122, 123
    Spanish wartime trips, 50, 121–124, 122, 123, 124, 125, 127, 128
    suicide, father's, 80
    suicide of, 202–203
    tough-guy image, 17, 35, 37, 42, 57, 62, 73, 85, 109, 112, 122, 123, 136, 143, 146, 159, 164, 166, 204
    wounds, effects of, 26–27, 35, 40
    writing habits, 64, 76, 78, 80
    writing style, development of, 34, 42–43, 50, 54
Hemingway, George (uncle), 14
Hemingway, Grace Hall (mother), 3–4, 6, 7, 8, 12, 14, 16, 19, 27, 34, 35, 38, 40, 71, 77, 80, 90, 166, 174, 178, 204

Hemingway, Gregory Hancock "Gigi" or "Gig" (son), 92, 135, 139, 144, 159, 160, 164, 169, 174, 178, 204
Hemingway, Hadley Richardson (wife), 39–41, 42–45, 46, 47, 48–49, 50, 51, 58–59, 60–61, 63, 65, 67, 68–69, 70–71, 72, 73, 75, 82, 98, 99, 116, 162, 193
Hemingway, Henny, 174, 183, 188
Hemingway, John Hadley Nicanor "Bumpy" (son), 54, 56, 59, 61, 64, 65, 67, 68, 69, 72, 73, 80, 84, 86, 95, 96, 98, 129, 134, 139, 143, 158, 159, 160, 165, 204
Hemingway, Leicester Clarence (brother), 13, 145, 204
Hemingway, Madelaine "Sunny Jim" (sister), 5–6, 80, 204
Hemingway, Marcelline (sister), 3, 5, 204
Hemingway, Martha Gellhorn (wife), 114–115, 116–123, 127, 129, 130, 131, 133, 135–138, 141–145, 147, 158, 159, 161
Hemingway, Mary (aunt), 11
Hemingway, Mary Welsh (wife), 143, 145, 148–149, 153, 157, 159–165, 167–171, 173–176, 179, 181, 183, 184, 187–188, 190–192, 194–202, 204
Hemingway, Patrick (son), 78–79, 80, 81, 91, 92, 135, 139, 144, 159, 160, 164, 165, 172, 174, 178, 183, 188
Hemingway, Pauline Pfeiffer (wife), 60–61, 65, 67, 69, 70, 71, 72–73, 78–79, 80–82, 86–87, 90, 92, 94–95, 98–99, 106, 107, 111–115, 124, 126, 127, 129–131, 162, 165, 176, 178, 181
Hemingway, Tyler (uncle), 16, 20
Hemingway, Ursula (sister), 5, 204
Hemingway, Welloughby (uncle), 11
Herrera, Dr. José Luis, 160, 165
Hickok, Guy, 44
Hitler, Adolf, 99
Hollywood, 121, 164, 178, 191
Horton Bay, 6, 19, 34, 35, 38, 40
Hotchner, A. E., 166, 171, 172, 175, 189, 192, 198, 199, 204
Hotel Florida, 117, 119, 122, 123, 181
hunting, 84, 86, 94–95, 100–102, 113, 114, 130, 131, 134, 139, 164

I

Indonesia, 138
In Our Time, 54, 58, 59, 64, 65, 70
International News Service, 47
Islands in the Stream, 176
Italy, 23–31, 34, 40, 45, 49–50, 72, 73, 76, 94, 99, 143, 166–169, 172
Ivancich, Adriana, 167, 168, 169, 172, 173, 174, 176, 204

J

journalism, 16, 19, 20, 21, 27, 38, 47, 50, 152–159
Joyce, James, 44, 103
Joyce, Jane, 139
Joyce, Robert, 139

K

Kansas City Star, 16, 19, 20–21, 37, 38
Kenya, 92, 100, 179, 181, 188
Ketchum, Idaho, 130, 139, 194, 195, 198, 199, 201, 202, 204
Key West, Florida, 76–78, 80, 82–83, 88, 90, 92–96, 104, 106–107, 109–111, 113–116, 121, 124, 127–129, 131
Kilimanjaro, Mount, 100
"Killers, The," 68, 70, 161, 164
Kurowsky, Agnes von, 27–31, 34, 76, 81

L

Lanham, Colonel "Buck" Charles, 148–150, 153–155, 157–159, 161, 164, 166, 197
Lausanne, Switzerland, 48
Lewis, Sinclair, 88
Life magazine, 145, 166, 176, 195, 197, 198
Liveright, Horace, 58, 59, 60, 64, 65
Loeb, Harold, 54–63, 71, 82
Longfield Farm, 6, 12, 14, 19, 35
Look magazine, 181, 188, 191
Luckner, Count Felix von, 142

M

McAlmon, Robert, 49, 50, 51, 52, 57
MacLeish, Archibald, 58, 69, 70, 71, 75, 79, 84
Making of Americans, The, 56

Mason, Jane, 92, 94, 97, 106, 112
Men at War, 140
Men without Women, 73
Montana, 87, 90
Monte Grappe, 31, 33
Moveable Feast, A, 193, 201
Murphy, Gerald, 67, 69, 94, 104
Murphy, Sara, 67, 69, 94, 104
"My First Sea Voyage," 8
"My Old Man," 48, 49

N

Nairobi, Kenya, 100, 101, 181, 183, 187, 188
Nazis, 99, 115, 117, 136, 141
New Masses, 110
New Republic, 97
New York, 21, 31, 53, 54, 59, 60, 65, 79, 80, 84, 86, 92, 95, 103, 109, 116, 121, 124, 126, 127, 128, 130, 131, 133, 135, 136, 138, 159, 164, 170, 172, 176, 178, 179, 192, 197, 199
New Yorker magazine, 166, 170, 173
New York Herald Tribune, 73
New York Sun, 33
New York World, 69
Nobel Prize, 190
"Nobody Ever Dies," 128
Norquist, Lawrence, 84, 90, 114
Norquist, Olive, 90
North American Newspaper Alliance, 114, 116, 125, 126, 127

O

Oak Park, Illinois, 3, 4, 5, 6, 13, 14, 19, 20, 33, 38, 54, 79, 80
O'Hara, John, 173
Old Man and the Sea, The, 175, 176, 178, 179, 190, 191
Ordoñez, Antonio, 179, 181, 192, 196–199
Ordoñez, Carmen, 197, 199
Ordoñez, Cayetano, 62–64, 179
"Out of Season," 50

P

Pamplona, Spain, 51, 53, 57, 61, 62, 69, 81, 91, 179, 196
Paris. *See* France

Pearl Harbor, 139
Percival, Philip, 92, 100, 101, 111, 181, 182, 183, 184, 188
Perkins, Maxwell, 65, 70, 71, 73, 79, 80, 81, 83, 84, 90, 92, 93, 95, 96, 101, 114, 121, 123, 128, 133, 134, 157, 165
Petoskey, Illinois, 4, 36, 37
Pfeiffer, Gus, 70, 72, 78, 87, 90, 92
Pfeiffer, Mary, 69–70, 79, 84
Pfeiffer, Paul, 69–70, 79, 84
Pfeiffer, Pauline. *See* Hemingway, Pauline Pfeiffer (wife)
Pfeiffer, Virginia, 60, 68, 71, 79, 84, 90, 98
Piggot, Arkansas, 69, 78, 79, 84, 87, 88, 92
Pilar (boat), 104, 105, 106, 109, 112, 121, 138, 142, 144, 160, 167, 169, 173, 174, 179, 190
Pinehurst Cottage, 5, 6, 13, 35, 41
PM tabloid, 135, 138
Porter, Katherine Anne, 103
Pound, Ezra, 43, 48, 49–50, 54, 56, 60, 99, 193
Pulitzer Prize, 179

R

Rawlings, Marjorie, 112, 123
Red Cross, 21–23, 21–31, 25, 27, 61
Richardson, Elizabeth Hadley. *See* Hemingway, Hadley Richardson (wife)
Ritz Hotel, 153, 157, 159, 171, 181, 192
Ross, Lillian, 166, 170, 172, 173
Royal Air Force (RAF), 144, 146, 148, 157
Russell, Joe, 93, 96, 97, 112

S

Samuelson, Arnold, 105
Saunders, Bra, 77, 78, 93, 104, 110
Saunders, Willard, 109
Saviers, Dr. George, 199, 201, 202
Schio, Italy, 23, 25, 30, 45
Scribner, Charles, 175, 176
Scribner's Magazine, 69, 70, 81, 84, 107, 110, 123, 134
Sea in Being, The, 174
Sea When Absent, The, 174
Shipman, Evan, 95, 96

"Short Happy Life of Francis Macomber, The," 111, 161

skiing, 49, 50, 59, 65, 71, 75, 82, 168, 172

Sloppy Joe's Bar, 93, 107, 114, 116

Smith, Bill, 16, 19, 34, 35, 40, 61, 62

Smith, Katy, 16, 19, 39, 82

"Snows of Kilimanjaro, The," 101, 113

Spain, 50–51, 53, 57, 61–64, 68, 69, 73, 81, 91, 95, 97, 98, 113–114, 116–117, 119, 121, 122–125, 127–128, 145, 150, 179, 189, 192, 195, 196, 199

"Spanish Earth, The," 119, 121

Speiser, Maurice, 95

Spiegel, Clara, 131

St. Louis, Missouri, 39, 40, 60, 78, 115, 129, 143, 166

Steffens, Lincoln, 48

Stein, Gertrude, 42, 43, 44, 50, 51, 52, 54, 56, 65, 96, 193

Stewart, Donald Ogden, 57, 58, 59, 62, 92, 121

Strater, Henry "Mike," 48, 49, 50

suicide, 26, 80, 173, 176, 202–203, 204

Sun Also Rises, The, 63, 64, 65, 67, 69, 70, 71, 72, 73, 82, 90, 181

Sun Valley, Idaho, 130, 134, 135, 139, 162, 163, 164, 165, 166, 194

T

Thiesen, Earl, 181, 183, 191

This Quarter, 58, 60, 61

Thompson, Charles, 77, 94–95, 99, 101, 102, 183

Three Soldiers, 46

Three Stories and Ten Poems, 52, 54, 58

To Have and Have Not, 121, 123

Toronto Star, 37, 44, 46, 47, 51–53, 54, 56, 145

Torrents of Spring, The, 64–65, 67, 69

Tracy, Spencer, 179, 191

transatlantic review, 54, 56, 57

Turkey, 46–47

Turkish-Greek dispute, 47, 48

Twelfth Brigade, 122

Twenty-second Regiment, 148, 158, 159

Twysden, Lady Duff, 61, 62–63, 71, 82

U

U-boats, 141, 142

"Undefeated, The," 60, 70

"Up in Michigan," 36, 43, 60

V

View Farm, 129

W

Wallace, Ivan, 84, 85, 86, 94

Walloon, Lake, 4, 5, 6, 7, 12, 13, 19, 35, 38

Walsh, Ernest, 58, 60, 61

"Way You'll Never Be, A," 94

Wellington, "Pete" C. G., 120

Welsh, Mary. See Hemingway, Mary Welsh (wife)

Williams, Taylor, 130, 139

Wilson, Edmund, 58, 71, 88, 110

Windemere Cottage, 4, 5, 6, 8, 11, 13, 14, 16, 19, 38, 40, 41

"Wine of Wyoming," 84

Winesburg, Ohio, 40

"Winner Take Nothing," 93, 99, 101

Woolf, Virginia, 73

World War I, 16, 21–31, 142, 159

World War II, 128, 167, 192

Wyoming, 79, 83, 84, 94–95, 113–114, 129, 135, 163, 164

Y

Yearling, The, 112

Z

Zaphiro, Dennis, 181, 182, 183, 189

Zaragosa, Spain, 70, 122, 192